Fred Secombe

HOW GREEN
WAS MY CURATE

—

Illustrated by Maxine Rogers

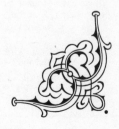

MICHAEL JOSEPH
London

MICHAEL JOSEPH LTD
Published by the Penguin Group
27 Wrights Lane, London W8 5TZ, England
Viking Penguin Inc., 40 West 23rd Street, New York, New York 10010, USA
Penguin Books Australia Ltd, Ringwood, Victoria, Australia
Penguin Books Canada Ltd, 2801 John Street, Markham, Ontario, Canada L3R 1B4
Penguin Books (NZ) Ltd, 182–190 Wairau Road, Auckland 10, New Zealand

Penguin Books Ltd, Registered Offices: Harmondsworth, Middlesex, England

First published 1989

Typeset in 11/13pt Sabon by Goodfellow & Egan Ltd, Cambridge
Printed and bound in Great Britain by Richard Clay Ltd, Bungay

A CIP catalogue record for this book is available from the British Library

ISBN 0 7181 3250 5

To my wife Sandra
without whose help and encouragement
this book would not have been written.

HOW GREEN
WAS MY CURATE

5 BOOKS FOR £5—
OTHERS IN THE STOCK ROOM

'I hope you have better luck with this parish than you've had in your first one.' My mother's parting words echoed in my head as the Paddington train pulled out of High Street Station, Swansea on the first Saturday in June 1945.

Standing in the corridor, jammed between a burly Welsh guardsman and a lanky aircraftsman, my five-foot-seven made me appear like the ungenerous filling in my Auntie Edna's sandwiches. The two servicemen carried on a conversation over my head while I mused on my mother's words.

My first curacy had been a disaster. Burning with enthusiasm I had gone from college to St Matthias, Swansea, only to have the fires quenched by the wettest of vicars, who had never had a curate before. In the eighteen months I wasted there, I learnt nothing from a man who was more interested in being outside his parish than inside it. Now I was going to an elderly priest who had trained many curates.

Canon R. T. S. Llewellyn MA, Oxford (Third Class Theology and a boxing blue) was Vicar of Pontywen (population six thousand) in the Western Valley of Monmouthshire. According to his advertisement in the *Church Times*, there were three churches, two in the town and one in the countryside, recently linked with Pontywen.

At Newport Station, I made my escape from the scrum in the corridor and carted my case over the railway bridge to a side platform where an empty train was waiting to carry passengers up the Valley. I collapsed into a seat. Just as I was beginning to think that I would be alone on the train, a swarm of humanity appeared from nowhere. Not for the first time, however, I found that my clerical collar made me an outcast from society. While every other compartment was filled, I remained in splendid isolation all the way to Pontywen.

My new Vicar met me as I got off the train, inspecting me as if he were a farmer at a cattle mart, eyeing a possible purchase.

'You don't look well, young man,' he rasped. 'Nothing wrong with your health, I hope.' Obviously he did not wish to 'buy a pig in a poke'.

'I'm fine, thank you, Vicar,' I said. 'We tend to be pale as a family.'

He grunted.

'Isn't it sad that a clerical collar frightens people?' I commented pompously. 'I had an empty compartment the whole of the journey from Newport.'

'When you are my age, Secombe,' he breathed 'you'll be glad of the empty compartment.'

He was a little man, in his seventies, about five-two at most and quite unprepossessing. His face was pushed to one side by an enormous goitre. Beady blue eyes, set in a florid countenance, would look into the soul of anyone he met for the first time, as I could testify from the short interview I had had with him some weeks previously.

We approached the ticket barrier where a motley throng of servicemen on leave plus miners and their wives, back from a trip to Cardiff, fought their way out of the station.

'Put your case down and wait until the mob has gone,' the Vicar commanded, standing aside from the mêlée like Napoleon surveying the battle of Waterloo.

'Carry on, Secombe,' came the next order as the last of the 'mob' disappeared past the ticket collector. I stood to attention, picked up my luggage and marched behind the little man out of the station.

For a man of his age he was remarkably agile. I found it difficult to keep up with him on our walk up a steep hill, to the Vicarage.

'I must admit, I feel more than a little excited,' I gasped.

He stared at me.

'I mean about starting my curacy in Pontywen,' I explained.

He grunted for the second time. It was many years since he had been excited about anything or anyone, especially his wife who looked as if she had been born in a refrigerator.

This was evident when she opened the door to us at the Vicarage, which was ideally situated between the church and the public cemetery. Mrs Llewellyn's welcoming smile was like a silver plate on a coffin.

Tea was served on a refectory table in the large dining-room. The three of us sat at some distance from each other. Conversation was at a premium. Semaphore would have been a more appropriate means of communication.

After a sparse meal of spam, boiled potatoes and pickled cabbage, followed by Vicarage-made scones anointed with a scrape of margarine, the Vicar led me to his study, a gloomy vault of a room. Dozens of bookshelves filled the walls and the smell of furniture polish pervaded the room. I was motioned into a leather armchair which was still fresh from Mrs Llewellyn's attentions. It was cold to my posterior. He sat behind a large desk, almost disappearing from sight.

Silence reigned. I began to feel very uncomfortable. Suddenly he pounced, like a Gestapo officer toying with his prey.

'What prayers do you use at the bedside of the sick?' he demanded.

I was dumbstruck. My previous vicar was expert at funerals but rarely present at the bedside of the sick. If he did visit anyone who was ill, he would be more likely to discuss rugby than the state of the invalid's soul.

'I'm afraid I have never said prayers with the sick,' I stammered.

'Never?' he thundered.

'I – I'm afraid not.' I feared for his blood pressure. He was purple.

'You have been ordained eighteen months and never said prayers with the sick.' The canon was incredulous.

I thought it advisable to remain silent.

'On Monday afternoon,' he said, 'you will come visiting with me. We shall visit both the sick and the whole.'

There was a further hiatus.

The old man was as conversational as a Trappist monk. He contemplated the ceiling whilst I ruminated on the possibility that I had jumped out of the frying-pan. Then another inquisitional bullet whizzed in my direction.

'Preach from notes or a fully written sermon?'

I was afraid that he was going to ask me that question. Mainly from indolence rather than a desire to communicate with my audience face to face, I had begun to preach without a scrap of paper in front of me. My first vicar was not concerned about my method of preaching as long as I could get up into the pulpit and say something for a quarter of an hour. It was evident that my new employer would be more demanding.

'I did – er – preach from notes but – er – lately I have been using no notes at all.'

'At your age, no notes at all?' he bawled.

'Of course, Vicar,' I went on quickly, 'if you want me to write out notes or a full sermon, I shall do so.'

'*If* I want you? Of course I want you to write out your sermon. Bring your sermon written out for next week when you come here on Monday morning. In the meantime, tomorrow you will have to preach without notes at St Padarn's at eleven o'clock. At Evensong you will take the service here in the Parish church and I will preach.'

By now I felt like a schoolboy who had not done his homework rather than the self-assured Curate who had caught the train at Swansea.

As I was wondering what the next examination question would be, the little man jumped to his feet and said, 'Well, you had better go to your lodgings now. I'll take you along to Mrs Richards. We'll have a long talk on Monday morning.'

We made our way through drab terraces to Mount Pleasant View. Anything less pleasant it would be difficult to imagine. It was a one-sided row of brown stone cottages, huddled perilously on a hillside and facing a vista of coal tips on the other side of the valley. Mrs Richards lived in number thirteen. Ominous, I thought, as the Vicar banged imperiously on the knocker.

The elderly, smiling lady who opened the door appeared far from ominous. Dressed in black, in mourning for a husband who had been dead twenty years, she was so short that she made even the Vicar look tall. Her white hair was neatly arranged in a large bun which bristled with hairpins. She looked like an amused version of Queen Victoria.

'So this is our new Curate.' She smiled with her eyes as well as her mouth, unlike Mrs Llewellyn.

4

'I won't come in, Mrs Richards,' said the Vicar. 'See that he's in church in good time for the eight-thirty service, won't you?'

'Well, Vicar, if I could cope with his ancestor Mr Price, I'm sure I can with this young man.' She smiled at me again.

Arthur Price, my predecessor at Pontywen, had been a fellow student at college where he had been noted for his devotion to his bed. On many occasions he had come to the college chapel for early morning service, with his pyjamas underneath his cassock and a camouflage of talcum powder to hide his unshaven countenance. After a couple of years of Canon Llewellyn, he must have left the parish with a nervous breakdown.

The house was spotless. I was given the front parlour as my room. Two empty brass shell-cases from World War One gleamed on either side of an immaculately black-leaded fire grate. They reflected the evening sun which was hovering over the distant coal tips. A large armchair, with a flower-patterned cover, filled one corner of the bay window, facing a flower-pot stand, complete with aspidistra, in the other corner.

After unpacking my case in the little back bedroom, I brought my college books down to my room and arranged them on the empty bookshelves alongside the fireplace. Reposing on the crocheted tablecloth was a tray with a cup and saucer and a plate containing two pieces of what my mother called 'cut and come again cake'. There was an atmosphere of warmth which compensated for the chilly reception at the Vicarage.

A gentle tap on the door announced the presence of Mrs Richards, plus small teapot.

'Are you settling in, Mr Secombe?' she enquired.

'Very well, thank you. I'm sure I shall be very comfortable.'

'There's nice,' she said. 'I've brought you some tea to go with the cake. By the way, don't be put off by the Vicar's aptitude. His bark is better than his bite.'

It was evident that every conversation with Mrs R. would provide gems of which Mrs Malaprop would be proud.

After tea and the delicious homemade cake, I decided to

get on with my sermon for the vicar. It was good to know about his bark. Perhaps as time goes on, I thought, he will appreciate my desire to do my best.

I had written three paragraphs about the parable of the prodigal son when there was an almighty commotion in the other room followed by a loud knock on my door.

'Mr Secombe, come at once.' Mrs Richards sounded frenzied.

I dashed to the door to find my landlady in a state of shock. Her normally pallid face was a whiter shade than white against the stark black of her widow's weeds.

'What's the matter, Mrs Richards?' I asked anxiously, expecting some dreadful tidings.

'It's a — ' She paused before she could say the dreaded word. 'It's a mouse.' She whispered the word in terrified confidentiality. 'It's under the grate in the middle room. I was reading the *South Wales Echo* when this thing ran over my foot and into the fireplace; I tell you, I nearly transpired. I can't go back in there till you've got rid of it.'

My instant reaction was one of great relief that nothing catastrophic had occurred. But the relief was followed by apprehension that I was expected to get rid of the mouse. Physical bravery has never been my forte and I detested encounters with rodents.

Some six months previously I had been involved in a staring match with a rat. Our theological college had been evacuated to the remote Cathedral City of St David's after a landmine had destroyed the College buildings in Cardiff. Most of the students were housed in the old Canonry which had been unoccupied for some time. We slept in improvised dormitories in very cramped conditions; our uncomfortable single beds were interspersed with small chests of drawers, each containing our belongings and any titbits our loving parents had given us to supplement our monastic diet. I had been given a box of cheeses by my mother as a special treat for that term.

During the nights we had heard noises in our room, scuttlings behind the skirting board, and the ominous contact of teeth on wood. But as yet we had not seen any animal. Then in the early hours of one morning I was awoken by a noise very near me. I looked up as I lay rigid in my bed to see a rat above me, on top of my chest of drawers. To borrow a cliché from Ethel M. Dell, 'Our eyes met and lingered.'

This shared experience must have been of brief duration. To me at the time it seemed an eternity. I do not know how long it seemed to the rat but he was the first to break off the encounter. He turned tail and darted behind the chest of drawers. I let out a yell which shattered the calm of the Cathedral Close. As a result, rat poison was administered efficiently – only to produce such an odour some weeks later that the floorboards had to be taken up and the corpses removed.

Now Mrs Richards was asking me to face a mouse which could turn out to be a rat. Perhaps it was a large rat. In any case, how was I to kill it? I had once seen a student, a son of the farm, corner a rat in the fireplace of the dining room at St David's. He attempted to kill it by stamping on it, and it jumped for his throat. Fortunately for him, it missed, but it cleared the dining room in no time.

'How am I going to get rid of it?' I said plaintively. 'There's nothing here to do it with.'

She scurried to my fireplace and produced a poker. 'There you are,' she said urgently. 'That'll get rid of it.'

She thrust the poker into my hand and propelled me towards the door of her living room.

I have never been less anxious to enter any room – and that includes a dentist's surgery. I stood outside for a few moments with my hand on the knob, took a deep breath and then flung open the door as if to surprise some unseen enemy, wielding the poker like Errol Flynn in one of his swordsman roles.

Mrs Richards slammed the door shut behind me. I was alone with the creature whatever it may be. I was in semi-darkness and had to make my way to the electric light switch. I collided with a dining-room chair and knocked it over in my haste to put on the light.

'Have you got it?' said the voice behind the door anxiously.

'I've knocked over one of your chairs, that's all,' I shouted. I hoped I was not expected to give a running commentary. It was enough to cope with the mouse or whatever it may be.

I switched on the light.

'Can you see it?' enquired the voice without.

'I've only now put the light on,' I said. 'I think it's better if we both keep quiet. It's the only way to get rid of it.'

'Right you are,' said Mrs Richards. 'I'll be quiet as a mouse.'

There was no answer to that.

I waited a while to see if I could hear anything – to no avail. Obviously the mouse was living up to its reputation.

On tiptoe I inched my way past the table to the fireside. There was an oxidised metal curb as a surround and inside that, some ornamental tiles on which reposed a fire-stand, complete with tongs, poker and shovel. The grate was empty and through the bars one could see into the ashpan. If Mrs Richards was right, the mouse was inside the ashpan. I decided to tap the grate with the poker to see if there were signs of life. Sure enough, when I did so there was a rustle from inside.

The moment for decisive action had arrived. With fast-beating heart and some heavy breathing, I knelt at the side of the grate with the poker raised in my right hand. Then with a flash of inspiration I realised that the shovel from the stand would give me a better chance of swatting the rodent than a poker. I took the shovel and used the tip of the poker to withdraw the ashpan.

A small house mouse, even more terrified than I, cowered in the corner of the ashpan. I brought down the shovel with a mighty blow and only succeeded in knocking over the fire-stand. Meanwhile the frantic rodent escaped over the side of the ashpan with the speed of lightning and disappeared under the sideboard.

'Are you all right?' enquired Mrs Richards, in a tone of concern.

'I'm all right,' I shouted, 'and so is the mouse. It's gone under your sideboard somewhere.'

'You'd better get it from there,' shrieked my landlady. 'I don't want to have it nesting in my drawers.'

'There's no fear of that,' I said reassuringly, speaking on behalf of the mouse. 'I'll try to get it again, but we've got to be quiet.'

This time there was no reply. My message had gone home.

I waited on my knees with shovel poised, for the mouse to make the next move. It was a very patient mouse. The minutes ticked by and my weapon-wielding arm began to ache.

If this stalemate continues, I thought, I shall not be able to move my arm before long, let alone bring down the shovel on the pestilent thing.

Suddenly there was a scuttle along the skirting board in the direction of the door behind which Mrs Richards was sheltering.

I threw the shovel at the offending creature. Needless to say, it missed but it struck the door with a noise like the crack of doom.

'What's that?' cried Mrs Richards.

'I missed,' I said.

'Hurry up, please,' begged the old lady. 'I want to go to bed but I can't while that mouse is there.'

I picked up the shovel and advanced towards the empty grate to see if the mouse had run back there. By now my fear of the fast, darting creature had given place to a determination to destroy it.

I peered into the space under the grate, now devoid of the protection of the ashpan. There, hiding in a far corner, was my prey.

I knelt down, counted up to three, and lunged with the shovel. There was a contact with living flesh which sent a shiver down my spine. It was all over. The poor creature was

crushed to death. I let out a yell which was composed of relief and revulsion.

'Is it all right?' came the plea from Mrs Richards.

'Yes, come and see,' I said with a note of triumph, like a midwife inviting an anxious father into the labour ward.

Gingerly she entered the room. I held out the shovel on which reposed the insignificant remains of the cause of the alarm.

'Ugh!' she said with a shiver – as if she were surveying the body of a dragon which had been about to devour her. 'Thank you, Mr Secombe, I don't know what I would have done without your resistance.'

2

I was in the pulpit of the tin tabernacle dedicated to Saint Padarn, surveying the packed congregation who had come to inspect the new curate. It was during the hymn before the sermon. This was being sung with half an eye on the hymn book and the other eye and a half on the preacher. The June sunshine poured through the windows and was beginning to roast my audience. Embarrassment combined with the temperature to produce rivulets of perspiration visible and invisible upon my person. Suddenly, I was aware of the tall figure of Mr Bertie Owen, Churchwarden, who was making ticktack signs to me from the back of the Church. I decided to look down at the Bible on the lectern with the idea that if I ignored him, he would stop his antics. To no avail. When the congregation were seated and I had launched into my sermon, the strange hand signs continued. I decided to look at him and nod my head. It had the desired effect. A satisfied smile spread across his florid countenance and the semaphore ceased.

The next minute he paraded down to the front pew, pushed a little lady to the side, stood on the seat and opened the window at the top. This procedure was repeated another five times until all the windows were open. My sermon was being delivered to the backs of the congregation's heads. They were all turned to watch Bertie balancing on the seats with one leg up in the air like a circus performer.

His tasks done, he sat down on a chair at the back and smiled at me indulgently, nodding his head at the end of every sentence I uttered. This continued for about five minutes when he decided I had gone on long enough. He got up from his seat and went across to a cupboard on which he reposed the Collection plates. Next he proceeded to deliver the four receptacles to various members of the congregation with a whispered instruction to each of them.

By the time he had got to the fourth whisper, my patience was exhausted. I stopped my sermon and stared at him. Aware that the flow of words from the pulpit had dried up, he raised his head to find me glaring at him. 'Sorry, Curate,' he boomed. 'Carry on, we're all with you.'

That was the *coup de grâce* for me. 'And now to God the Father,' I said and announced the Collection hymn. The four sidesmen took the Collection while I prepared for the next part of the service. Next I took the alms dish ready to receive the offerings of the congregation. The four men stood to attention at the back, looked at each other's feet to see that they were in step and marched down the aisle. To my astonishment they were followed by Bertie who was bringing up the rear minus a collection plate but with the aplomb and military bearing of a Regimental Sergeant Major.

The sidesmen emptied their takings on the alms dish in turn. I was about to offer up the money when Bertie took a few quick steps forward.

'You got the number then,' he said.

'What number?' I asked.

'You know – the number of communicants – eighty-seven. I gave you the signals.' His tone was reproachful.

'Oh yes, thank you,' I said and turned to the altar for the presentation of the offerings. As I finished the prayer, Bertie produced a not so *sotto voce* 'Quick turn', and the quartet of sidesmen performed a military manoeuvre, worthy of the Changing of the Guard. It was evidently one of the highlights of every service.

The same military precision was present when the time came for the administration of the consecrated bread and wine. Bertie strode down the aisle to the front pew and had each benchful of communicants coming forward by numbers. When it came to the back pew, Bertie joined on at the end to make himself the last communicant.

As I was about to administer the chalice to the kneeling

Churchwarden, there came another of his whispers. 'Do you want any help?'

'What help?' I asked.

'I drink what's left of the wine if it's too much for the parson,' he said eagerly.

'I'll manage, thank you,' I replied, handing him the chalice.

He was just about to pour the remainder of the wine down his throat when I snatched the silver cup from his grasp.

Bertie looked hurt. He could see an end to a much cherished perk.

By the time the service was over he had recovered his composure. He strode into the vestry before I had time to finish the prayer with the choir. Hardly had the 'Amen' died away before he said loudly.

'I see you found the copy of *Macbeth* I left on your desk.'

The man was full of surprises.

'What copy of *Macbeth*?' I asked in bewilderment.

'You know,' he said. 'The one you used in the Service.'

The mystery deepened.

'I'm very sorry, Mr Owen,' I replied, 'but I did not do any such thing.'

'Of course you did,' he answered, looking at me as if I were deranged. 'You sang from it when you took it to the altar.'

I was about to reply that I had never taken a copy of Shakespeare into Church and I would certainly never have put it to music. Then it dawned on me. He was referring to the Merbecke setting of music for the Communion Service.

'Oh!' I said. 'You mean Merbecke.'

'That's it,' he replied. 'I knew it was something to do with Shakespeare.'

There were some ill-controlled snorts of hilarity from the choir who had listened in silence to this vaudeville patter. Evidently Bertie was unaware that he was a source of amusement to them. The laughter passed over his venerable white locks.

'Come on boys that's enough,' one of the basses said. He was a tall, wiry man in his thirties, with more hair in his nostrils than on his head. 'I'm Idris the Milk – not here in the mornings normally, but 'ad time off to come special for this service.' His handshake was a bone crusher.

After the choir had disrobed, he introduced me to them, giving a job description of each member. They were: Mr Mills, a steel worker and his two sons; Mr Beyon, a fat, elderly insurance man; Mr Paxton, a retired miner with blue scars on his face and a rose in his button-hole; Mr Golding a working miner in his thirties, unscarred and with no rose, and lastly, Idris the milk's son, Percy, a fresh-faced ten year old.

The ladies of the choir had sat in the two front pews, led in singing by Mrs Collier, the organist's wife. She was a small, thin, bespectacled lady, who had more than her share of vocal power. Her main rival power-wise was a short, plump lady who attracted my attention by putting her dentures into her handkerchief before each bout of singing.

Bertie Owen was counting the collection on a table strewn with books and other impediments. He was assisted by the other churchwarden, Charlie Hughes, an elderly man with a deaf-aid.

'What did you say the silver was, Charlie?' enquired Bertie with the extra loud voice that the insensitive use with the hard of hearing.

Charlie jumped a few inches, took off his glasses, and confronted Bertie.

''Old on, you dull bugger!' he exclaimed. 'Sorry, Mr Secombe,' he said, realising my presence. 'That's the second time he's put me off. Now I've got to start all over again.'

'Can I help in any way?' I asked. 'That's not your job, Curate,' said Bertie. 'Charlie and me will sort it out. You get off home for your dinner.'

I picked up my case and made my way out of the vestry only to be confronted by the bevy of females from the two front rows, led by the organist's wife. They presented a daunting spectacle. None of them appeared to be under fifty.

'We've already met, haven't we?' said Mrs Collier. 'Well here are the rest of the choir ladies. This is Mrs Annie Jones,' The erstwhile toothless soprano thrust herself forward and revealed a gleaming set of dentures.

'You'll find us a very friendly lot, very homely, if you know what I mean.' She purred and fluttered her eyelashes in an effort to do a Mae West. I had difficulty in extricating my hand from her sweaty grasp.

One by one, I was introduced to the other choir ladies but by the time the last introduction was over, they were all still there, as noisy as excited schoolgirls. It was becoming claustrophobic.

'Coming, Mr Secombe,' Idris the Milk came to my rescue with a powerful basso profundo which drowned the twitterings.

Outside the church, he said, 'I thought you was in need of a bit of help. The choir ladies always get a bit excited when we get a new curate.'

'Thank you, Idris,' I said. 'I thought I'd still be there at teatime. By the way, I hope you don't mind me calling you Idris.'

'Everybody calls me that. You'll understand when I tell you my surname. It's Shoemaker. My grandfather was German, and came to the Valleys to get a job in the mines as a blacksmith. The poor old man was interned in the First World War. After that, he changed his name to Shoemaker, the English word for what it was in German.'

'It's just as well, Idris, for your sake, in the war that's just ended.'

'I was born and bred in Pontywen. It wouldn't have made any difference to the people here what my name was – unless, of course, it was Hitler.' His laughter at his own joke echoed through the Sabbath quiet of Church Terrace.

'If you don't mind my asking,' I said, 'how is it that you are not in the Forces or down the mines?'

'It's my feet,' he replied. He pointed at his very large feet which were splayed like Charlie Chaplin's. 'They are a bit deformed. I was disappointed I couldn't join up, but the wife wasn't. You must come and meet her. She had to leave Church early to cook the dinner.'

'I'd love to,' I said.

'Come and have fish and chips with us on Friday night. Mr Price used to make it a date.'

'I'll be pleased to do the same,' I replied. 'Thank you very much indeed.'

When I opened the door of thirteen, Mount Pleasant View, the aroma of Sunday dinner caressed my nostrils. It smelt like home and not like my last lodgings. There my landlady had another lodger who had spent some time in India. The result was that we had curry with everything. It was one of the many reasons why I left the parish.

'Do you mind having dinner in the middle room with me?' enquired Mrs Richards nervously.

'Not at all,' I replied. 'I'll be glad of the company.'

She beamed and said, 'I can see we're going to get on with each other – just like a house that's got a fire.'

The joint of lamb was a generous size for two people with ration books – especially since my landlady had received mine too late for Sunday dinner.

'How did you manage to get such a nice joint, Mrs Richards?' I asked.

'Well, I had a word with Mr Protheroe, the butcher. I've known him since he was a boy in his father's shop. Between you and me and the doorpost, I think he gets some meat from that old market that people talk about.'

'The black one,' I said.

'That's it,' she went on. 'I don't know where it is, but I'm very glad of the bit extra when I want it.'

It looked as if number thirteen Mount Pleasant View was going to be a haven of contentment.

At five-thirty p.m. prompt, I left the house for my first evening service at the parish church. It was a large towerless construction, grime-ridden and devoid of character. The roof at the west end was surmounted with a turret in which was suspended a single bell. Wartime regulations had condemned it to a merciful silence. Now, as I approached the church, my ears were assaulted by its unmusical clang rapidly repeated by a frenzied Quasimodo.

I was met inside the church door by a thin, wizened man in his sixties, clad in a cassock, who introduced himself as 'Hezekiel Evans, lay-reader.'

'H'I shall be reading the first lesson. You will be reading the second,' he announced.

'Fine,' I said. 'I never like to be the opening act.'

My feeble attempt at a witticism withered in his uncomprehending stare. He was a very serious servant of God.

He led me to the Vicar's vestry. It was a gloomy, bare vault, sparsely furnished with a large wooden table which served as a desk, an iron safe and a couple of stiff-backed clerical chairs. On one wall hung three faded photographs of past vicars, also stiff-backed and suffocating in their high collars.

'Put your clothes on this 'ook.' He pointed to one of three on the opposite wall to the photographs. 'The hother two belong to the Vicar. H'I'm afraid h'I 'ave to join the *oi polloi* in the choir vestry.'

It was obvious that the opening act was going to be hilarious. I unpacked my case, divested myself of my jacket and suspended it upon the appropriate hook, as the Vicar appeared in the doorway.

'Ah, Secombe,' he said breathily. 'I see Evans has shown you your hook. I suppose he complained that he had to dress in the choir vestry.'

'More or less,' I replied.

'More than less, I expect,' grunted the Vicar. 'Now then. You take the Service and read the second lesson. Give out the hymns and the psalms. I will read out the notices for the week and preach. You sit opposite me on the organ side. You will find a book of prayers in your desk.'

I felt like saying 'aye-aye sir' and saluting smartly. Instead I said meekly, 'Thank you, Vicar.'

The organ pealed out the voluntary impressively, quite unlike the harmonium playing its hurdy-gurdy notes in the tin tabernacle. At five fifty-nine p.m. precisely, a well drilled choir of men and boys lined up outside the Vicar's vestry with Mr Evans, at the rear, looking important with his blue-ribboned badge of office over his surplice.

A strange nasal whine emerged from the Vicar. It was the vestry prayer. As its discordance ended with an uncertain 'Amen' from the choir, we wheeled into action through the vestry doors. Into the church we went, led by a burly adolescent, brandishing a processional cross.

Through the west window the evening sun streamed, illuminating a crowded congregation, each of whom appeared to be eyeing me with keen interest. As I approached the step to my desk on the organ side, my foot made contact with the bottom of my cassock instead of the floor. My body jerked forward and my nose was in imminent danger of collision with the ornamental carving at the side of the desk. I clutched at the top of the desk for support, knocking over the massive prayer book which had reposed there until then. There was an almighty bang as it fell to the floor. When I stooped to pick it up, the front cover came away in my hand. I reappeared from behind the desk with the front cover in one hand and the rest of the prayer book in the other. The congregation and choir seemed amused. The Vicar was not. Then there was an awful silence. The organ had stopped. Everybody was standing and nothing was happening. I looked at the Vicar. He glowered and pointed at the hymn board.

In my embarrassment, I had forgotten that I had to announce the hymn. There was no time to look for the list. I peered at the board.

'Hymn number one hundred and forty-five,' I said hastily. The elderly chorister next to me elbowed me in the ribs.

'That's the psalm,' he hissed. 'The hymn is three hundred and forty.'

'I beg your pardon,' I stammered. 'Hymn number three hundred and forty – the three hundred and fortieth hymn.'

The Vicar's goitre had grown considerably by now. I was afraid it might explode.

After that awful beginning, all went well. I announced the correct psalm and, when that finished, sat down to listen to the first lesson from Ezekiel Evans.

''Ere beginneth the sixth chapter of the book of the prophet Hisaiah.' The aitches disappeared from their usual place and popped up elsewhere.

'Hand one cried hunto hanother hand said – 'Oly 'oly 'oly, his the Lord of 'osts.' The lesson ended with a dramatic flourish – 'Halso h'I 'eard the voice of the Lord saying, 'oom shall h'I send, hand 'oo will go for hus? Then said h'I, 'ere ham h'I' – a theatrical pause – 'send me.'

Whatever happens, I said to myself, the second lesson is bound to be an improvement on that. I began to fancy myself as John Gielgud as the fifteenth chapter of St Paul's First Epistle to the Corinthians got under way. All went well until I arrived at the words, 'what advantageth it me ...' John Gielgud could have dealt with it. I failed abysmally after three attempts, coughed and went on to the next sentence.

My début in the parish church was turning out to be a fiasco. I heaved a sigh of relief as I finished reading the prayers without a mistake. All that was left of the service was the sermon and that was not my responsibility. Canon Llewellyn fell to his knees and said a short prayer to himself as the rest of us sang 'Love Divine'. Then the little man ran up the steps of the pulpit and almost disappeared inside its depths.

I remembered a story about a diminutive lecturer I had known in my student days. He used to stand on a box in the pulpit in order to be visible. One day he was invited as a guest preacher to a large town church in South Wales. It was a very deep pulpit and there was no box.

When the time for the sermon arrived, two inches of forehead appeared above the pulpit ledge.

'I take my text', proclaimed the lecturer, 'from the eighth chapter of the Gospel according to St John, part of the twelfth verse, "I am the light of the world".'

Whereupon, it is said, a wag at the back of the church said very audibly, 'Then would you mind turning up the wick, please?'

I was so engrossed in the memory of this story that it took me some time to realise that the congregation were beginning to titter very faintly. The reason for the amusement was not two inches of forehead, but the fact that the preacher, whose eyes were closed, was addressing the stained glass window at the side of the pulpit. Carried away on a tide of eloquence, he continued to lecture the images of St Peter and St Paul, on the subject of the ten commandments.

Mrs Llewellyn, in the front pew, reserved for the Vicarage, opened and shut her handbag several times – to no avail. She decided to cough violently. Her beloved was oblivious of the loud coughs and the quiet laughter from the congregation. For a full quarter of an hour he harangued a stained glass window.

'And now to God the Father,' he said, at the end of his

sermon, opening his eyes and looking at the two Saints who had heard it all before several times.

His face turned purple. He wheeled around saying, 'Son and Holy Spirit. Amen.' The Canon's eyes met those of his wife. He died a thousand deaths. Sunday dinner that day must have been a silent repast under arctic conditions.

'Well,' said Mrs Richards as she brought me a nightcap of cocoa. 'How have you enjoyed your first Sunday in Pontywen?'

'It has been like the curate's egg,' I replied. 'Good and bad in parts. I enjoyed this morning, but this evening at the parish church was terrible. I'm afraid I made a mess of things.'

'Go on, Mr Secombe,' said the old lady. 'You were very good. I could hear every word. It was the Vicar who made a mess of things – preaching to the window with his eyes shut like that.'

'Mrs Llewellyn was very annoyed,' I laughed. 'She tried to draw his attention.'

'She'll give him attention tonight all right.' Mrs Richards folded her arms. 'Between you and me and this doorpost, that woman treats him like a little boy. It was bad enough when she was his housekeeper, but since they're married, it's twenty times worse.'

'How long have they been married?' I asked.

'Five years,' replied my landlady. 'He'd been a bachelor all his life till then and she'd been a spinster. It's too late to tie a knot then.' She paused.

'Another thing,' she went on, 'if you don't mind me saying, you'll have to watch your steps with her. Now she's Vicaress, she thinks she rules the rooster.'

'I hope she doesn't think she's going to rule this rooster,' I said. 'Perhaps I had better change my text for next Sunday's sermon to, "No man can serve two masters".'

'Funny you should say that,' Mrs Richards replied, 'that's what Mr Price said the day that he left.'

As a child attending morning service with my mother, I was under the delusion that the vicar was greatly concerned about anybody who vomited. Every Sunday morning he would pray for 'those who were sick'. Then one day in answer to my question about the vicar's anxiety about people who vomit, my mother informed me that Mrs Evans, number ten in our street, needed the cleric's prayers because of her pneumonia, not her vomiting.

'Why doesn't he say "ill" instead of "sick"?' I asked.

'Because,' said my mother, 'that's how you tell God that somebody is ill.'

'Doesn't God know what "ill" means?' I persisted.

'Stop asking questions,' commanded my mother. 'You know what "sick" means in church now.'

That sentence ran through my mind as I was taken by the Vicar for my lesson on how to minister to the sick. After the previous day's happenings he was not in the solicitous frame of mind which I would have thought necessary for a bedside manner. Evidently Mrs Llewellyn had not appreciated his attempt at driving tuition.

The walk to number ten Balaclava Street was like a stroll in a monastery garden. The Vicar spoke not a word while the expression on his face deterred any words from me.

We stopped outside a terraced house where the paint had begun to peel from the window frames some years ago, leaving most of the wood rotting and unprotected against the inroads of a polluted atmosphere. The unwashed curtains in the front room downstairs window were drawn, revealing a number of places requiring needle and cotton.

A loud bang on the door by the use of a rusty knocker announced our presence. The door was opened by a grey-haired old lady, unkempt and wearing a filthy pinafore over a dress which reached floor level.

'We've come to say prayers with Amos,' declared the Vicar.

We were ushered into the smelly front room where the sun was fighting a losing battle with the drawn curtains. The sole furniture was an iron bedstead with unpolished brass knobs and with a commode alongside the bed. Amos was evidently in the final stages of cancer.

'How are you today?' demanded the parson.

'About the same,' whispered Amos.

'I'm going to say prayers.'

It sounded more like a preface to the nine o'clock news than an invitation to prayer.

The invalid closed his eyes while his vicar produced a small book and thumbed through its pages. When he found what he wanted, he read the couple of prayers with as much warmth in his voice as a professor of mathematics addressing his students on the quantum theory.

Amos opened his eyes at the second Amen and looked at me through heavy eyelids.

'Is this the new Curate?' he asked.

'This is Mr Secombe,' announced my superior. 'He'll be coming to say prayers with you next week.'

'Cup of tea, Vicar?' Mrs Amos had poked her head around the half-opened door.

'No, thank you, Lizzie,' replied the Vicar, to my great relief. 'We have to be on our way.'

The dust-laden air of Pontywen outside was like champagne after the stench of the front room.

We paid three more visits to the 'sick', at which the little book reappeared with the same two prayers being featured. Each time the captive on the sick-bed was ordered to receive the spiritual medicine: two prayers to be taken once a week.

After our fourth visit, the Vicar said, 'Now then, Secombe, you know what to do. Never go without saying prayers. A sick bed is not a social occasion. You may borrow this book for your afternoon visiting at the hospital, page twenty-two, numbers three and four.'

On my way back to number ten Mount Pleasant View, I opened the book which was intended to be my life-line at the bedside. The fly-leaf revealed that the prayers for all occasions had been written by a bishop at the end of the last century. In 1945 the prayers were as dated as a Kitchener poster.

'How do I get to the Hospital?' I enquired of Mrs Richards.

'It's a real climb to get there,' she said. 'At the back of the church, you go up Evans Terrace, turn right into Aberystwyth Avenue, by the slaughterhouse, and then up the hill again into Hospital Road. The hospital is at the end of the road. There's a beautiful panama when you look from the top of the steps.'

'I've got to see Mrs Waters, Councillor Waters' wife, and Miss Howells,' I informed her.

'Oh,' she replied, 'I knew Miss Howells, Top Shop, was in. She's been very ill with her stomach. Sceptic ulcer, they thought, but it sounds much worse than that. Fancy Mrs Dai Spout being in. I hadn't heard anything about that.'

'Who is Mrs Dai Spout?'

'She's Councillor David Waters' wife. Everybody calls him Dai Spout because he never stops talking. She hardly ever comes to church, mind, but he's chapel when he goes – not often, like her. They've got one boy, Aneurin – big for his age but not very bright they say.'

Armed with this information, I set out for Pontywen Hospital in the early afternoon sunshine. Mrs Richards was right. It was a long climb, especially on a hot summer's day. The reward was a panoramic view; a mixture of green-topped hills, unconquered by the Industrial Revolution, with valleys scarred with coal tips or belching yellow smoke from works dedicated to the war effort.

The hospital was an ugly Edwardian building built of the same brown stone as the slaughterhouse further down the road and the terraced houses on the hillsides.

On entering the gloomy portals my nostrils were assailed by the smell of so much antiseptic that I was convinced that no germ could survive once over that doorstep.

I decided that first I should visit the elderly spinster before I faced the spouse of the local VIP. A large board inside the entrance hall indicated the directions to the various wards. Carefully noted in my parson's pocket book was the information that Miss Howells, the elderly lady, was in Evan Morgan Ward while Mrs Waters, the councillor's wife, was in the Princess Royal Ward, in keeping with her status.

Following the indicating arrow on the board, I proceeded down two corridors, only to find myself outside what was obviously the maternity ward, by the noise of bawling babies emanating from it. Convinced that an elderly spinster would not be on the other side of that door, I tried another corridor. This time I found the Evan Morgan Ward.

For a minute or two I stood outside summoning up enough courage to enter. I counted up to ten and pushed open one of the doors. Facing me was the entrance to the ward, and before that, on either side, three more doors. There was no one in sight.

We had been instructed at the theological college that no person entered a ward without getting the Sister's permission first. On one of the doors was emblazoned the words, 'Sister's Office'. My timid knock received no answer. I knocked again with a slight increase in strength. To no avail. All was quiet. The minutes ticked by. What little courage I had left evaporated. I pushed my way through the doors out into the corridor.

Back in the entrance hall, I consulted the board for the Princess Royal Ward. It was on the opposite side of the hospital and on the first floor. I arrived outside the ward doors without a mishap and, feeling more relaxed, went inside without counting up to ten. Boldly I went straight to the Sister's Office and knocked firmly on the door. I heard the scrape of a chair on the floor but there was no answer to my knock. My nerve was giving way. I tried again, with a gentle tap rather than a knock.

'Come in!' barked an impatient contralto. On entering, I discovered a plump, grey-haired lady in blue uniform seated at a desk and poring over a sheaf of papers. She did not look up.

I stood waiting.

She continued the study of her dossier.

'Yes?' she demanded, her head still bent over her desk.

'I am the – er – new Curate of Pontywen,' I said nervously.

'Are you?' she snapped, continuing to look at the desk as if it were a fascinating case, requiring acute observation. I joined her in staring at the desk, mesmerised and speechless.

'Well?' she enquired, addressing the desk once more.

'Please may I see Mrs Waters,' I said, feeling not unlike Oliver Twist in the presence of Mr Bumble.

'Second bed on the right,' she told the desk.

'Thank you, Sister,' I breathed in reply and made a quick exit.

Now I had to venture into the ward, painfully aware that as soon as I pushed open the doors, many a female face would turn in my direction. And so it was. There seemed to be hundreds of women in bed. One of these, in the second bed on the right, was my first sick visit.

With my eyes firmly fixed on the floor, as if it were the Sister's desk, I made my way to Mrs Waters. When I looked up I saw a lady in her late forties, as far as I could judge.

The councillor's wife was thin-faced, with sharp features. Her nose and her chin were in danger of meeting. She had attempted to stem the ravages of time by dyeing her hair a colour which wavered between pink and red.

'I'm the new Curate,' I said to her.

'Pleased to meet you,' she replied.

'What is wrong with you?' I asked.

She blushed the colour of her hair. There was a momentary silence before she whispered, 'Internal'.

They should have taught us in college never to ask a lady patient what is wrong with her, I thought.

'Are you – er – coming along all right?' I asked.

'Oh, yes,' she replied, having recovered her composure. 'I had the operation last Tuesday and I'm having the stitches out tomorrow, with a bit of luck. I should be home this week some time.'

'Pleased to hear that,' I said and lapsed into silence. I was conscious of several pairs of eyes concentrating on me.

'I'm glad you've come,' said Mrs Waters. 'We don't come to church very often. My husband 'as a lot of meetings on a Sunday, with the Party, you know. So we don't get a chance to get to the services. But I am very keen that my son should be confirmed.'

'Well, I tell you what it is,' she continued. 'I want him to have good references when he leaves school. That's the only way to get on, and it'll be a big 'elp, if he can put down that he was confirmed.'

There was no answer to that doctrinal view of confirmation. I stood, incredulous and speechless.

'How long 'ave you been in Pontywen then?' she asked.

'Three days,' I replied.

'You'll see us in church one of these days,' she said, with a complete lack of conviction.

At this stage, I thought I had better turn the social occasion into a sick-bed exercise.

Nervously I felt in my pocket for the book of prayers, only to produce my parson's pocket book. Not for the first time that week, I began to feel hot and bothered. There was a hiatus in the conversation which Mrs Waters showed no sign of continuing. It was obvious that she wanted me to go.

Feeling in my other pocket for the all-important book, I stammered, 'Er – would you like me to – er – say prayers?'

The effect on Mrs Waters was devastating. She went white with fright.

''As Sister told you something I don't know?' she enquired, looking into my face.

'No! No!' I said quickly. 'It's just that – er – I thought you might like to have a prayer.'

'Thank you all the same,' she replied, breathing a sigh of relief. 'I can say my own prayers. I don't need nobody to say them for me.'

'If you don't mind,' I said, 'I'd better be going. I'm supposed to be at a meeting at three o'clock.' I did not tell her that it was a meeting with Miss Howells in the other ward.

'Thank you for coming,' she replied.

By now there were three nurses in the ward, engaged in various duties. Two of them were together with a patient two beds away from Mrs Waters. They were enjoying a quiet giggle and I had a deep suspicion that I was the cause of the merriment.

I decided on a quick exit. The highly polished floor accelerated the speed. I slipped and skidded towards one of the beds. I clung to it, jarring a startled patient and preventing myself from falling. The two nurses exploded into peals of laughter. The ward door swung open and the dragon appeared.

She stood at the entrance with her hands on her hips.

'What's going on here?' she demanded.

I felt I had to give an explanation before she would allow me through the doors.

'I'm afraid I – er – slipped and just saved myself from falling,' I explained.

'Your job is to save others from falling,' she said severely. 'Nurse James, Nurse Williams, come and see me in my office.'

I was sorry for the girls, who looked as if they were on their way to the scaffold.

'It must have looked very funny,' I said, in defence of the two nurses.

'I don't care how it looked,' retorted the Sister. 'Nurses are supposed to be in control of themselves.' However, there seemed to be a considerable diminution of her outrage. I had an idea that her bark was worse than her bite. At least, I hoped so for the sake of the girls.

Back out in the corridor, I heaved a sigh of relief. My first sick visit was over. Admittedly it was a baptism of fire but I had come through it unscathed, apart from a few dents in my ego and a slight strain in my left wrist.

I braced myself for ordeal number two and made my way back to the Evan Morgan Ward to see Miss Howells. Nonchalantly, I made my way through the outer doors and went to the Sister's Office. This time, my knock was answered by the opening of the door. A tall blonde Amazon of a Sister looked down at my five foot seven.

'Can I help you?' she said briskly.

'I'd like to see Miss Howells, please,' I replied.

'By all means,' said the Amazon. 'The ward is free.' With that, she retreated into her office, closing the door. How kind, I thought, compared with the monster in the Princess Royal.

Confidently, I pushed my way through the ward doors – only to find my confidence vanish in a trice. There was no nurse in the ward and I had no idea what Miss Howells looked like. Not for the first time that afternoon, I stood silent and nonplussed. The multitude of bed-bound females surveyed me as if I were someone newly arrived from outer space.

'Young for a reverend, isn't he?' said an old lady in the first bed on the left hand side.

' 'Oo d'you want, love?' asked another elderly patient.

'Miss Howells,' I said, feeling like Daniel in a den of lionesses.

'She's down by here,' came a voice from the far end of the ward.

As I made my way to the distant bed, with an occasional skid on the polished floor, I became increasingly embarrassed.

A middle-aged lady, sitting up in bed, adorned in a pink woollen bed-jacket, pointed to a recumbent figure in the bed opposite.

'That's her,' she said. 'I think she's asleep.'

I went across to the bedside of Miss Howells. She had almost disappeared inside the immaculately folded straitjacket of bedclothes. Only her forehead, surmounted by carefully combed grey hair, was visible.

'She've 'ad a bad night,' commented the lady with the pink bed-jacket.'

'Perhaps I had better not disturb her,' I said.

'I expect she'd like to see you, love.' The elderly occupant of the end bed, alongside Miss Howells, sat up and offered this advice, from a mouth which had caved in. Her false teeth reposed in a glass of water on her locker.

She leaned over and shouted, 'Miss Howells!'

To no avail. Miss Howells slumbered on.

Her neighbour was about to indulge in a double forte effort to arouse her.

'Please don't bother,' I interjected quickly. 'I'll come and see her later this week.'

'I'll tell 'er you've called.' It was the pink jacket again. 'Where's your church, Vicar?' she asked, using an assumed 'posh' accent.

'He's not a Vicar,' said the toothless one knowingly. 'He's a Curate.'

'Would you mind letting 'im speak for 'imself?' replied

pink jacket in cutting tones. 'You're always interfering.'

'It's only because you are so ignorant,' retorted Miss Howells' neighbour.

' 'Oo do you think you are?' demanded pink jacket whose temper had given her face a colour which clashed with her bed attire. 'If you was younger, I'd deal with you.'

'This ward was peaceful till you came, wasn't it, Mrs Evans?' persisted the toothless one, appealing to her next but one neighbour over the recumbent form of Miss Howells.

Mrs Evans pretended to be asleep.

I decided to escape quickly.

'Good afternoon, ladies,' I said, and made for the door, even more crimson-faced than the owner of the pink jacket. The argument was still continuing as I left.

As I passed the Sister's Office, the door opened and the Amazon emerged.

'You've not been long,' she said.

'I'm – er – afraid she was fast asleep and I didn't like to wake her,' I replied.

'Come back in with me,' said the Sister, 'and I'll wake her for you.'

The thought of going back into the ward was more than I could bear.

'I couldn't stay in any case,' I fibbed. 'I have to go to a meeting. I'll come again.'

'As you please,' she said and disappeared into what appeared to be a broom cupboard.

Once outside the hospital, I felt a tremendous sense of relief – almost as if I had escaped from a prison. The euphoria began to evaporate as I made my way down Hospital Road.

'What do I say to the Vicar if he asks me about the saying of the two obligatory prayers?' I said to myself.

He would have ordered Mrs Waters to have the spiritual treatment with as much authority as the ward Sister.

I decided that, if he asked me about my spiritual administrations, I would indulge in a white lie. After all, I did ask her whether she wanted prayers. As far as I am concerned, I told myself, the prayers were said.

When I got back to my digs, Mrs Richards met me as soon as I opened the door.

'Quick!' she said. 'Amos Evans is dying. They can't find the Vicar. He's out in the car with Mrs Llewellyn somewhere. It's number ten Balaclava Street.'

'I know,' I replied. 'I was there this morning.'

'It'll be a merciful disease,' she shouted as I ran down the steps.

My heart was beating painfully by the time I reached the death-bed – more from fear of the unknown than the exertion of running. I had never seen anyone die.

The death rattles were audible outside the closed door of the front room. Inside, they were frightening in their intensity, accentuated by the silence of the death-watch.

Lizzie was sitting, holding her husband's hand and staring, intently at his open-mouthed, toothless face. His half-lidded, upturned eyes gleamed white above his yellow, sunken cheeks.

'Would – would you like me to say a prayer?' I stammered the question out of a dry mouth.

'Yes, please,' she whispered, addressing Amos, not me.

I paused. The rattles in the throat subsided and the breaths became frighteningly intermittent.

'Heavenly Father,' I began. My mind went blank as I waited for the next breath. The smell of death and decay was overpowering. I felt sick.

Suddenly, a breath exploded out of the body, convulsing the whole frame. It was its last breath. Amos was at rest.

'Amen,' intoned a large, fat lady, standing at the bedside, apparently dressed in a black tent. She made the sign of the cross and mumbled something in Latin.

Lizzie was still holding her late husband's hand and gazing into his face.

The fat lady turned to me. 'I'm Bridget Barry from next door,' she said, in an accent common to Dublin, not Pontywen. Her voice softened as she spoke to the widow. 'He's with his maker now, my dear. Why don't you go into the other room with the Minister, while I see to him?'

I put my arm around Lizzie and led her gently from the death-bed.

She was still in a daze, when I left her. Seated on a kitchen chair by the empty grate of the living-room, she was being

31

attended by two neighbours and plied with an unwanted cup of tea.

I made my way down Balaclava Street, feeling as dazed as Lizzie. As I was about to reach the end of the terrace, the Vicar's car turned the corner. He was so intent on his errand of mercy, that he did not see me. It was just as well. I could not have faced an interrogation about my administration of the last rites.

When I reached the privacy of my own room, I burst into tears – probably as much from shock as compassion. After all, I had only known the parted couple a matter of hours.

'Thank you for administering the last rites to poor old Amos,' said the Vicar. We were disrobing in the vestry after the Wednesday morning service.

'It's a good thing you were back from the hospital. You'd better keep that book of prayers, Secombe.'

'That's very kind of you, Vicar,' I replied.

'The funeral's next Monday. Now then, you had better see Jones the gravedigger about a funeral tomorrow. He has a habit of digging the grave at the last minute. Number five, Thomas Row. It's just below where you live.'

Thomas Row was a terrace of decrepit cottages, all devoid of numbers as far as I could see. The occupants of most of the houses in Pontywen preferred to remain anonymous.

Half-way up the street, an old man was sitting in the doorway of his house, enjoying the morning sunshine and his pipe.

'Excuse me,' I said. 'I'm looking for Mr Jones, the grave-digger.'

'Full-Back, you mean.' He giggled and dribbled down his chin. 'I don't think anyone has ever called him Mr Jones.'

'Why is he called Full-Back?' I asked.

The old man wiped his chin with the back of his hand. 'Well, it's like this. He's very proud of the fact that he once played full-back for Pontywen. Mind, that was at the beginning of the First War. They only played five matches and packed it in because they couldn't find enough players. He never played again when the War was over.'

'Why was that?'

'He wasn't any good, that's why. Too lazy. He used to be counting the daisies when he should have been keeping his eye on the ball. He was the only full-back Pontywen ever had who was tying his boot laces while the opposition was scoring a try. Always been lazy.'

'Could you tell me which is his house? I've got to see him about digging a grave.'

'Gravedigging's the only job he's ever had – if you can call it a job. That and poaching rabbits. He's the best poacher for miles around. You should see his ferrets.'

'Which house did you say was his?'

'And betting. I've never known a man bet like him. Horses, dogs, anything. He'd bet on the date of his granny's funeral.'

'Excuse me,' I said firmly. 'I have to get back for my dinner. Can you tell me where he lives?'

'Next door but one – though I don't know whether he's in. 'He could be out with the ferrets.'

'Thank you – I'll go and find out.' I was moving away as I said it, in case I was trapped for the next hour.

'You the new Curate?' persisted my informant.

'Yes,' I shouted from outside the open door of number five.

'Who's that?' came a voice from inside number five.

'I've come about the grave.'

A short, unshaven whippet of a man appeared in the somewhat insalubrious passage. He was clad in a brown jacket with holes at the elbow and once grey flannels, tucked inside filthy wellington boots. Two rusty safety pins were being used to repair rips in his trousers. On his head was a battered, greasy trilby. A toothless grin split his cadaverous face as he spotted my collar. He extended a grubby hand.

'So you're the new Curate.' His toothlessness distorted his speech.

'Play rugby?' he asked.

'No, I used to play soccer.'

'You should play rugby. A man's game. I used to play full-back for Pontywen.'

'So I've heard.'

'They all call me Full-Back.'

'I'll do the same then,' I said. 'The Vicar is asking if you've got the grave ready for tomorrow.'

His eyes gleamed and his smile almost reached his ears.

'What d'you think?' he said excitedly. 'The grave number is A three and there's an 'orse running at Newmarket tomorrow called A Three. Thirty-three to one. I'm going to 'ave two bob on it.'

Evidently nobody in Thomas Row answered questions at the first time of asking.

'The Vicar wants to know if you have got the grave ready for tomorrow.'

'It's 'arf done. It'll be finished by tonight.'

'I'll see you tomorrow,' I said. 'I'm taking the funeral.'

' 'Ope you bring me luck then.' The grin reappeared.

As I made my way past the elderly sunbather, he called out, ' 'E was in then.'

'Yes, thank you.'

'You taking the funeral?'

'Yes.'

'Whose is it?'

'Mr Mainwaring from Hafod Street.'

'Poor old Llew. Well it's a happy release. Been enjoying bad 'ealth for years. Talking about rugby, now there was a fine scrum-half.'

'I'm afraid I've got to go now.'

Don't let me keep you. All I 'ope is that the grave is dug properly. Mind, that will never 'appen as long as Full-Back is there. You'll find out.'

He pointed his pipe at me. I waved my hand at him and went off at a brisk pace before he could impart any more gratuitous information.

At a quarter-to-two next day, guided by Mrs Richards' directions, I made my way to Hafod Street. The Vicar had gone to see the bereaved earlier in the week. 'Take the service in the house and at the graveside. Gentlemen only,' he instructed.

There was no trouble finding the house. Groups of men in black, engaged in earnest conversation, surrounded the open door.

Forwards and three-quarters of long ago quietly recalled

the glories of Pontywen, when Llew Mainwaring was the tactical master at scrum-half. Most of the doors in the vicinity were open and gawping women with folded arms leaned against the lintels.

It was a sultry afternoon. In the distance black thunder clouds were beginning to build and faint rumbles disturbed the stillness. An elderly woman appeared in the doorway and called me inside.

A strong smell of disinfectant permeated the passage. I was ushered into the front room where the drawn blinds created a Stygian gloom. The furniture had been pushed to the walls to accommodate the expected crowd.

'I'll bring Mrs Mainwaring in now,' said the lady in black.

'Don't hurry her. There's plenty of time,' I replied.

I looked at my Bible and found One Corinthians Fifteen, the burial lesson. Then I turned to the prayer book and put the marker in Psalm Twenty-three.

Some minutes later, the widow was ushered into the room, looking red-eyed but very composed.

'Sorry about your trouble,' I said, holding her hand.

'Thank you for coming,' she whispered.

'I understand Mr Mainwaring had been ill a long time.'

'Yes, my dear,' she murmured. 'I know it's a happy release, but when you've been married forty years, it's hard.'

She sat down on a chair by the window. One by one the mourners began to move into the constricted space until eventually it was as full as the enclosure at a rugby international.

'We'll have to leave the door open,' said one of the men. 'There's still some in the passage who can't get in.'

There was the sound of a car door being closed outside.

'Can I get through, please, gentlemen?' a loud voice requested. A short, plump, red-faced, white-haired undertaker barged his way into the front room. His frock-coat smelt strongly of mothballs.

'Good afternoon, your reverence,' he said to me and shook my hand with a wet fish grasp. 'Pleased to meet you.' He turned to the widow. 'Do you want to see Mr Mainwaring before we screw him down?'

'No thank you, Mr Matthews. I've said goodbye.'

'Right, then,' he said. 'We'll go upstairs and bring him down.'

The undertaker pushed his way into the passage and called his minions to follow him upstairs.

I waited until they had closed the door of the bedroom. The heat in the room was intense. The combined odour of death, camphor and sweat was stifling. Thunderclaps exploded overhead.

'We'll start,' I announced, 'with the Twenty-third Psalm.'

I began to read the beautiful words. When I reached the verse, 'Yea, though I walk through the valley of the shadow of death', there was the sound of the door opening upstairs.

'Watch your end, 'arry,' said Mr Matthews loudly.

'Thou shalt prepare a table before me . . .'

'Feet first,' instructed Mr Matthews,' and careful of your end, Eddie.'

'But Thy loving kindness and mercy . . .' I intoned.

'Watch that bottom step Eddie,' said the undertaker.

'And I will dwell in the house of the Lord for ever.'

'Excuse us, gents.' Mr Matthews was now superintending the movement of the coffin through the passage.

The burial lesson was punctuated with instructions about passing the wreaths from the middle room to the hearse.

I was left in silence to read the prayers. There were a few suppressed sobs from the widow. As I came to the last 'Amen' a flash of lightning penetrated the twilight of the front room and was followed by the clatter of heavy raindrops. A massive crack of thunder shook the house. The seated women looked up in alarm at their men who would have to stand outside in the rain.

Mrs Mainwaring forgot her grief momentarily. 'Would somebody like to borrow Llew's umbrella? It's in the cupboard under the stairs.'

Immediately the tension was broken. Wives were suggesting that the funeral should be delayed until the rain stopped and the husbands were insisting that they were not afraid of getting wet.

Into the middle of the hubbub strode Mr Matthews in his frock-coat and now carrying his top-hat.

'I think it's passing over,' he declared.

This prediction was none too popular with the men in the passage and the middle room who were due to walk in front of the cars all the way to the churchyard. A strike appeared to be in the offing.

Suddenly the rain stopped.

'There you are,' said Mr Matthews. 'What did I tell you.' He sounded as if he was in direct contact with the Almighty.

He delved inside his frock-coat and produced a list.

'First car. Mr Evan Mainwaring, Mr David Mainwaring, Mr Graham Mainwaring, Mr Albert Mainwaring, Mr Hywel Mainwaring. Your Reverence will travel in front with the driver.'

The speed at which the undertaker got through the list would have beaten that of an auctioneer in full flight.

We moved out of the house to face an audience of a dozen or so women who, like the Duke of Plaza Toro in Gilbert and Sullivan's *Gondoliers*, 'enjoyed an interment'.

An inky sky was at variance with Mr Matthews' pronouncement that the storm was passing over. The cortège of burly men, all in black, lined up in twos and was inspected by the undertaker like a general reviewing his troops. He went to the head of the procession, put on his top-hat and moved off at an appropriate funereal pace.

Seated in the front of car number one, behind twenty men on foot, I began to speculate how long it would be before Mr Matthews would have to quicken his pace.

When we reached the end of Hafod Street, there was a nasty flash of forked lightning, followed by a deafening thunder-clap. Twenty heads turned upwards in complete unison. Mr Matthews went into top gear.

As the first large spots of rain began to fall, the undertaker was moving briskly towards the churchyard which was two streets away. Within seconds, a monsoon descended on the procession. None of the walking mourners wore a raincoat and there was just one umbrella in the first car to shelter Llew's five sons.

By the time we drew into the churchyard, the undertaker was setting a pace which was more appropriate to the Olympics than a funeral. The freshly-dug grave was at the bottom of a steep path. Full-Back Jones was standing under one of the trees which lined the churchyard wall. He waited until the cortège reached the bottom before venturing from his shelter.

A discussion about the umbrella was engaging the five sons of the deceased as I was about to alight from the front of the car. It was decided that the Curate should have its protection.

Greatly relieved, I held it aloft with my left hand while I tried to find the burial service in the prayer book with the thumb of my right hand. The rain beat a tattoo on the umbrella.

'The bearers, please,' shouted the undertaker.

Four big men emerged from the scrum of drenched mourners who were milling around the hearse and the two limousines.

I made my way to Llew's last resting place with my thumb stuck inside the prayer book at the right page. It was the most untidy grave I had ever seen. My elderly informant of yesterday was not exaggerating the extent of Full-Back's laziness. The grave was much less than six feet deep, as it should have been. To camouflage the lack of depth, bricks had been placed at the sides of the grave on which rested planks, ravaged by the effects of age and weather. To anyone standing on them, the grave appeared deeper than it was.

The undertaker snorted as he saw the shallow grave. He glared at Full-Back who was looking the other way.

The rain poured down relentlessly. Directed by the undertaker, the four stalwarts threaded the straps of webbing through the coffin handles, with water trickling down the backs of their necks as they did so.

'Lift,' ordered Mr Matthews.

They did so with some difficulty. Evidently Llew Mainwaring had been big for a scrum-half.

I stood on the short plank at the end of the grave. 'Man that is born of a woman has but a short time to live,' I intoned.

The four men moved on to the planks on either side of the grave, puffing as they carried their burden. Suddenly there was a loud crack like a pistol shot. The weight of the bearers plus that of the late Llew was too much for one of the ancient planks. The two men on the left hand side started to slide into the grave. As they went my short plank was disturbed and I joined them in the slide, with the coffin jammed between the three of us. The prayer book fell at the feet of the principal mourners and the umbrella crowned the headstone of a nearby grave.

For a split second, there was an awful silence. Like that at Cardiff Arms Park before a Welsh penalty kick.

The next I knew was that Full-Back had darted out from behind a gravestone and joined the undertaker in a combined rescue of the Parson.

Meanwhile there had been a swift effort by a number of breakaway forwards to support the two bearers who were still hanging on to the webbing straps attached to the coffin. The three of us were hauled to our feet, while the two bearers on the other side were purple in the face from the strain of holding the coffin.

Mr Matthews retrieved the umbrella and held it over me while one of the mourners handed me a sodden prayer book. I found the right page, now stained with mud.

The rain gushed down as I attempted to carry on where I left off. I have an inconvenient sense of humour. The sight of so many dazed faces surmounted by bedraggled hair was irresistibly comic. 'Man that is born of a woman,' I began

again. I strangled a giggle in a wet handkerchief. I coughed – a cough which was repeated so often for the rest of the service that the mourners must have thought I had contracted pneumonia.

As soon as I had finished, the undertaker said, 'I'll drop you at your lodgings on the way back. 'Ave a large drop of 'ow's-your-father when you get in.'

'A nice cup of tea will do me,' I replied.

'You know whose fault this is, your reverence,' he went on. 'That man Jones is a bloody amateur, if you'll pardon the expression.'

'I'll do that,' I said with feeling.

By the time I entered number thirteen Mount Pleasant View, I was in a sorry state. My robes were smothered in yellow, cemetery muck and my shoes were so muddy that I entered the house in my socks.

Mrs Richards appeared from her room as I stood in the passage with my shoes in my hand.

'Mr Secombe, fach, what have you done now?' she gasped.

'I fell in the grave,' I said. 'One of the planks broke.'

'It's that Full-Back's fault again. I don't know why the Vicar employs him. Most likely because he can't get anybody else, I expect. It was Dobson's choice,' she said with a sigh.

Later that evening when the rain had given way to pleasant summer sunshine, I went for a stroll down the main street of Pontywen. Outside the 'Lamb and Flag' I bumped into Full-Back who was about to enter its portals, still unshaven and still in his brown jacket, grey flannels and wellingtons, plus trilby. He smelt strongly of body odour and wet clothes.

To say that he looked miserable would be an understatement.

'Sorry about the plank,' he said.

'So am I,' I replied. 'Mrs Richards will have a hard job to get my surplice clean for Sunday.'

'You know that horse?' he enquired.

'A Three you mean.'

'Yes, that's the – er – blighter. I put two bob on her and she came in last.'

'It's not been your day, has it?' I said. 'I certainly did not bring you luck.'

It was some weeks later that I met him again outside the Lamb and Flag. He looked positively suicidal.

'You know that blessed horse, A Three?'

'Yes.'

'It ran at Epsom today at fifty to one. I didn't back it, of course. Blessed horse came in first!'

4

'I've still got another ten houses to visit,' I said to Mrs Richards over a lunch of ersatz sausage and mash. 'I had better get them done today before I see the Vicar tomorrow at the wedding. Well, it's only nine really. One of them is Idris the Milk and I'm going to have fish and chips with him and his missis tonight.'

'Mr Price always used to go to Idris on Fridays. He's very hospitalical – Idris. Where are the other houses?'

'Eight of them are in Colliers Street and the other in Melbourne Terrace.'

'Colliers Street is church rather than chapel. It's just two streets away from here down the hill and Melbourne Terrace is the next one down. It's very elect there. That'll be Mrs Powell.'

I decided to start on Collier Street with the grand finale among the 'elect'. Once again I was confronted with the problem of anonymous houses. The first number on my list was 'Mrs Bevan, number two'. I knocked on the numberless door of the second house.

The door was opened by a little girl of about four years of age, clad only in a filthy and extremely holey vest. She was smothered in several layers of dirt and had a recent application of raspberry jam on her cheeks. The child stared at me with a terrifying intensity. My self-confidence ebbed before her gaze.

'Will you tell Mummy that the – er – Curate has come?' That pastoral utterance sounded absurdly parsonical.

She ran down the oilcloth-covered passageway to the foot of the stairs. With a massive voice for one so small, she announced, 'Ma-am. The Cruet 'ave come.'

A dishevelled lady, in her early thirties, clattered down the carpetless stairs, a cigarette drooping from the corner of her mouth.

'Rita!' she screeched, 'get back in the kitchen. Running about with nothing on.'

This was decidedly unfair criticism, since she herself was clad in a pinafore and very little else.

'What do you want, love?' She addressed me as if I was the same age as Rita.

'The Vicar has sent me to see you,' I said, haltingly.

'What for?' She sounded suspicious.

By now I was convinced that I had made a mistake. 'Are you Mrs Bevan?' I asked.

'The other end of the street. Last but one, love.'

The door slammed.

I had started at the wrong end of the street. Mrs Bevan, at the other end, was highly amused that I had called on the lady in the pinafore and little else. Apparently she was in the habit of consoling herself constantly for the absence of her husband who was in the Eighth Army.

After three cups of tea and seven visits I arrived at my last house in Colliers Street. 'Mrs Annie Jones, number twenty-four.' The name rang a bell. When the door opened, it became an alarm bell.

I was confronted by the undentured soprano who had informed me on Sunday that they were 'a very friendly lot' in Pontywen. She was attempting to look very friendly with a fluttering of eyelashes and a mouthful of teeth. Face-powder and lipstick had been applied to such an extent that she could have been engaged as a circus clown. Her light summer dress was suspended over her large bosom like a flag draped over a balcony. A strong whiff of Soir de Paris floated in the air.

'I 'eard you was in the Street. So I was sure you wouldn't pass me by.'

Evidently the bush telegraph had been at work.

'You'd better come into the front room. I've got the kettle on ready for a cup of tea.'

The small front room was furnished with a Rexine three-piece suite, a couple of wicker-backed chairs, an occasional table and the inevitable flower-pot stand. Cheap ornaments vied with photographs for a place on the mantelpiece. All the ornaments bore the names of seaside resorts, a catalogue of holidays.

'Sit down on the settee,' she said, 'and make yourself at home while I get you a cup of tea.'

When she had gone out of the room, I sought in my mind for a plausible excuse to get away quickly.

She reappeared some minutes later with a tea tray which was covered with a lace doily, bearing two cups of tea and a plate of biscuits.

'I've put milk and sugar. I 'ope it's all right.'

'I'm sure it will be.'

'Take a biscuit. I slipped out and got them special when I 'eard you was in the street.'

I took two wafer biscuits.

'That's very kind,' I replied and took a sip of tea. It was strong and syrupy. My stomach heaved.

She went across to the mantelpiece, brought a photograph of a man in army dress and sat beside me.

'This is my 'usband,' she said. ''E's in India. I 'aven't seen 'im for three years.'

I looked at the head and shoulders of the soldier, his head surmounted with a forage cap and his face suitably solemn for one serving his country.

'You must miss him.'

'Oh I do! It gets very lonely without a man in the 'ouse, if you know what I mean.' She edged closer to me.

I knew what she meant. The room was becoming claustrophobic.

'Have you done a lot of singing?' I asked, desperate to change the conversation. 'I could hear your voice on Sunday.'

'There's kind you are to say that.' She did some more eyelash fluttering. 'I used to be in Pontywen Operatic before the War. I suppose it will start up again next year now that the War is over, except for those Japs.'

'I expect it won't be long before they give in. Then your husband will be home.'

'Yes,' she said flatly.

'By the way,' I went on, 'I'm fond of Gilbert and Sullivan.

I wouldn't mind forming a Church Society to do some of their operas.'

'Well there's exciting. I'd love to do one of those big parts in *Pirates of Penzance* or *The Gondoliers*.

I could imagine her, minus teeth, singing the part of beautiful Mabel in *The Pirates of Penzance*. The very thought was a nightmare. 'Secombe,' I said to myself, 'you've got to get out of here at once.'

'Good heavens,' I exclaimed as I looked at my watch. 'Is that the time? I've got to go.'

She pouted a droopy scarlet pout. 'We're only just getting to know each other,' she complained.

'I have to be back at my digs by four o'clock and I still have to go to Melbourne Terrace,' I said as I stood up sharply. 'Thank you for my tea and biscuits.'

'You've only drunk a mouthful,' she said.

'I'm sorry – but I really must go.'

'Well you must stay much longer next time.'

'I will, I promise.' I hoped next time would be in the distant future, the very distant future.

She stood on the doorstep and waved to me all the way down the street. More for the neighbours' sake than mine, I imagined.

Melbourne Terrace, obviously one of the more respectable streets in the parish, was one which would present a physical challenge to any postman. Each house, made of the dirty brown local stone, was approached by a series of steep steps.

I recovered my breath at the top of the steps of number eight and rapped the door with the gleaming brass knocker, the one bright object of the drab frontage. A minute later, as I was about to go away, a rattling of chains behind the closed door announced that the drawbridge was coming down.

To my astonishment there appeared Miss Betsy Trotwood, clad in mourning. According to my list she was, 'Mrs Powell (widow)'. A tall, thin, gaunt-faced, elderly lady with frizzy hair, she was dressed in a black frock more appropriate to 1845 than 1945. After a moment's silence during which she surveyed me from head to foot, she said, 'So you are the new Curate.' I realised how David Copperfield felt on first meeting his aunt.

'Come on in,' she ordered.

She led the way past the glass-panelled inner door into a hallway which reeked of polish and ushered me into the parlour. The brown Venetian blinds were drawn and the room had the smell of an unvisited museum.

Mrs Powell advanced towards the blinds and then with three quick tugs illuminated the place with the afternoon sunshine. For an old woman, she was very agile.

'Sit down,' was the next command.

I sat down on an uncomfortable leather-covered dining chair which adjoined a china cabinet near the door. On the walls were framed certificates and an enlargement of a photograph of a bride and groom, presumably Mrs Powell and the late Mr Powell. An aspidistra, in a brown pot, stood on a little wooden table in the centre of the bay window. There was an upright piano, standing stiffly to attention, against one wall, with a music stool on which were sheet copies of music, neatly stacked. Three other dining chairs and a leather sofa completed the furniture in the room. A square of carpet adorned with patterned brown leaves, surmounted the oilcloth on the floor. The fireplace was guarded by two brown and white china dogs. On the mantelpiece were several snapshots in heavy frames, and above it was a large oval mirror, suspended on a metal chain.

When Mrs Powell sat down opposite me, I felt that a cross-examination was about to begin. I was right.

'You from Swansea?' she asked.

'Yes. I've lived in Swansea all my life.' Then I added, 'Apart from being in College, of course.' I felt I had to be exact in every reply to this lady.

'Any brothers or sisters?'

'One brother who is in the Army and one sister who is working in a docks office,' I said.

The interrogation continued for some minutes. When she was satisfied with the catalogue of information she rewarded me with a cup of tea which was far too strong for my liking but which I dared not refuse.

'I suppose the Vicar has told you that I used to do all the children's operettas,' she said, with an air of self-importance.

'He did say something.' I prayed for forgiveness for one more white lie.

'Those concerts used to fill the hall. Very successful they were. The children loved them and all the parents used to come. The War stopped all that.' She obviously regarded Hitler as a spoilsport. 'Before I married Mr Powell, I was a schoolteacher, you see. I enjoyed teaching but I wasn't allowed to teach once I was married.' Evidently she regarded the late Mr Powell as a spoilsport, too.

Mrs Powell's cup of strong tea was the fifth I had drunk that afternoon and the accumulation of liquid inside me was at danger level.

Melbourne Terrace was three streets away from my lodgings. I could just about reach there in safety if I could leave Mrs Powell within the next few minutes. But how? She seemed set for at least another half hour's one-sided conversation; like Annie Jones.

A cold perspiration began to bespangle my brow. I wondered how many children in her class years ago had been in my predicament and had been afraid to ask for permission to leave the room. If I stood up to leave while she was in full flow it would appear extremely rude.

Deliverance came with a knock at the door. It was the baker, with a basket of bread. By the time Mrs Powell had reached the front door, I was in the passageway. As she was about to close the door on the baker, I blurted out, 'Mrs Powell, I've got to go, I'm sorry. I've an urgent appointment.' At least that statement was true.

I was down the steps in no time. Number thirteen Mount Pleasant View was soon in sight and a blessed sight it was. As I sat down to tea, I resolved that in visiting from now on, I would confine myself to two cups of tea per afternoon.

My rounds almost completed and just as I was about to visit Idris the Milk for my fish and chip supper, it began to rain; heavy, summer rain. Mrs Richards suggested that I might use the late Mr Richards' umbrella.

'I've kept it a long time. But if I keep it any longer the moths will get at it. Then it will be just a pink elephant. So you may as well use it.'

'Thank you, Mrs Richards,' I said. 'I appreciate your kindness. I'll buy myself one next pay-day.'

'Don't do that, Mr Secombe. As long as you are here, you can use it.'

The door of One Hillside Avenue, the abode of Idris the Milk, was wide open. I do not think I saw it closed during the whole of my stay in Pontywen. By the time I had closed the late Mr Richards' umbrella, the inner door at the end of the passage opened, and a flaxen-haired barefooted infant appeared, clad in a white nightdress. She looked like a cherub who had fallen out of a cloud. The vision stood staring at me and then ran back into the room. 'Mam, it's the poor bloody little Curate,' she proclaimed in a loud voice, for one so small. I realised I had already established an identity.

There was a brief silence within. Another figure emerged from inside. A somewhat flustered little lady, an adult replica of the cherub, hastened along the passage. 'Come on in, Mr Secombe,' she stammered. 'I hope you didn't hear what our Elsie said,' she added. 'We've been having trouble with her picking up bad language,' she explained.

Although it was the first week of June, a bright fire burned in the grate of the living-room. A large black-leaded kettle was singing gently from its perch on the glowing coals; gleaming in the firelight, a brass fender protected the coconut matting which stretched across the room in front of the fireside.

Elsie, a child of some three or four years, stood at the foot of the stairs on the opposite side of the room as if ready to make a quick escape from the impending parental wrath. Percy, the choirboy, was seated at the oilcloth-covered table reading his *Beano*.

'Percy, take Mr Secombe's coat and umbrella, and you, Elsie, off to bed. Say goodnight to Mr Secombe.' There was a ring of steel in the tone of voice. Suddenly I was enveloped in a pincer movement, with Percy on my left seizing my umbrella and Elsie on my right, proffering her rosebud mouth for a goodnight kiss, a picture of blue-eyed sanctity.

'Mind you don't get your nightie wet from my coat,' I warned.

'Let Mr Secombe take off his coat first,' said Mrs Idris, and then carried it plus umbrella, into the front room in a manner which Jeeves might have envied.

I picked up the cherub, who threw her arms round my neck and bestowed a rather wet kiss full on my lips.

'That'll do,' said her mother. 'And I don't want to hear a sound from upstairs.'

Elsie nodded her head in compliance, as if she were a model of obedience, and then ascended with haste.

'I hope you don't find it too hot.' Mrs Idris turned her big eyes on me. They seemed to occupy most of her face. 'It's Friday night, and that means bath night, see,' she said. 'Percy, come on, get ready. I'll warm up the water before you get in.'

So saying she produced a flannel cloth, caught hold of the handle of the big kettle, and proceeded into the scullery bearing her heavy load with all the agility of a champion bantam-weight lifter. The kettleless fire glowed with the intensity of a furnace in a steelworks. As the water poured into the tin bath, a cloud of steam floated into the living-room. I felt like a fully clad Eskimo trapped in a Turkish bath.

Percy dashed upstairs, taking his *Beano* with him, either for company or else in distrust of the Curate. His steam-bedraggled mother refilled the kettle, and mercifully reduced some of the heat in the living-room by replacing that receptacle on the fire, and sprinted into the scullery. Her son reappeared, wearing only his shirt to protect his innocence. His mother slammed the door. 'Don't forget to wash behind your ears,' she shouted.

'Don't stay standing up, Mr Secombe,' she said. 'Go and sit in that armchair over there. It's very comfortable. That's Idris's chair.' The chair adjoined the fireside.

I had no desire to be acquainted with Gehenna. 'If you don't mind,' I said, 'I'll sit here by the table where Percy was sitting. I expect Idris will want his own chair after a day's work.'

'Whatever you say, Mr Secombe,' she said. 'You make yourself comfortable anyway. I've got to tidy up after Elsie. Idris has gone down to feed Daisy and to put her to bed. He won't be long.'

She was amused at the look of bewilderment on my face.

'Daisy's the horse that pulls the milk cart,' she explained. 'Idris goes down every night to feed her and to see that she's comfortable.'

A few minutes later a heavy tread down the passage, accompanied by a couple of snorts worthy of Daisy, heralded the return of the breadwinner. He was a very wet breadwinner, clad in dripping oilskins – more like an advertisement for 'Skipper' sardines than for Evans the Dairy.

'There's good it is to see you,' he said to me, wiping a raindrop from the end of his nose.

'Before you sit down, Idris love,' said his wife, dipping into her purse, 'go round to Hugheses for some fish and chips, there's a lovely boy. Two cutlets, a tail, three twos and a penn'orth for Percy.'

Ten minutes later the three of us were enjoying the pleasures of freshly fried hake and chips, served on spotless plates on a spotless tablecloth, while young Percy retired to bed with his penn'orth wrapped in the *South Wales Echo*.

After supper, Idris reposed in his armchair by the fireside which was much reduced in heat by now. I brought my chair away from the table and sat the other side of the fire, facing Idris.

'Well,' said Idris, with a contented look born of a full stomach and a clear conscience, ''Ow you settling in?' His legs were stretched full and his eyes had an incipient glaze.

'All right, I suppose,' I said. 'It's been a very eventful week.'

There was no reply from Idris, whose eyelids were now fully closed. It was a picture of serenity. I felt it churlish to disturb him. I decided to look for pictures in the flickering of the dying fire. From inside the scullery came the familiar sounds of that most common of domestic chores – washing the dishes.

Suddenly the scullery door opened and Mrs Idris appeared, a few wayward strands of hair hiding some of the embarrassment on her face. 'Idris, you've done it again,' she scolded. Her dozing husband jerked upright into sensibility. 'He used to be like that when Mr Price the Curate was here to supper.'

'Sorry, Gwen,' said Idris.

'It's Mr Secombe you should apologise to, not me,' she said. 'And when you've done that, perhaps you'll help me to empty the bath.'

Idris shambled to his feet, like a tired sheepdog called to further duty. 'Very sorry, Mr Secombe,' he mumbled. 'Once I get near that fire I go out like a light, mun.'

He followed his wife into the scullery where the joint operation removed the tin bath and its contents into the yard outside. The water gurgled its way into the drain, in company with the rain which continued its relentless way. When the bath was emptied, there was a metallic clang as it came to rest on its end against the wall of the house.

My host, now wide awake after contact with the rain outside, went back to his chair, but refrained from sinking back into its alluring arms.

'What was you saying, Mr Secombe?' he said, all attention as if I were about to make a papal pronouncement.

With that there was an imperious knock on the outside door, followed by some earth-shattering steps down the passage, and another knock on the middle-room door.

'Come in,' said Idris, as if such intrusions on his privacy were commonplace. The door was flung open.

A wet giant in police clothes, cape over his massive shoulders and helmet in hand, stood dripping in the doorway.

'Daisy's got out, Idris, and she's running wild over the allotments. I can't catch the bugger.'

Idris was on his feet in a flash.

'I 'aven't long settled 'er down for the night, Will. Somebody must 'ave been messing about up there. Be with you now.'

'Do you mind if I come?' I asked. 'I have always had an urge to be where the action is happening.'

'The more the merrier,' said the police constable.

'You must be the new Curate. Will Davies 'ere.'

'I'm Fred Secombe.' He imprisoned my hand painfully.

'You don't have to go in all this rain, Mr Secombe,' interrupted Gwen Shoemaker as she emerged from the kitchen.

'It seems to be easing a bit now,' said P.C. Davies.

'In any case, I've got an umbrella. I'll be fine,' I reassured the little woman.

It was quite a walk to the scene of the break-out – uphill all the way. As a weather prophet P.C. Davies was as accurate as the undertaker the day before. Rain blew against us in sheets on the exposed hillside. The late Mr Richards' umbrella was little help.

'How much further?' I asked, between gasps.

'Almost there now,' said Idris, pointing to a row of corrugated iron sheds in the distance. I could see the allotments in their variegated patterns on the steep hillside.

'You've got a long way to go to get your horse every morning,' I said.

'You get used to it,' he replied. 'Every man to his job – mine with the milk cart, yours with the pulpit.' He stopped his philosophising and pointed. 'There she is. Look at her. She's feeding on somebody's greens by the look of it.' When we arrived at the allotments, the 'running wild' grey pony presented a picture of animal contentment, quietly enjoying an evening meal of young cauliflowers.

Idris started to make his way down the path towards Daisy.

'Wait a minute,' shouted P.C. Davies, 'you going to get a rope from the stable?'

'No need,' said Idris. 'She'll just follow me.'

He drew level with Daisy. As soon as she saw him, she ignored the rest of the cauliflowers and followed him up the path like a sheepdog.

'Well I'll be ...' P.C. Davies cut off his exclamation suddenly, as he remembered in whose company he was.

Daisy settled down in her quarters as if butter would not melt in her mouth.

'Somebody has untied the string that was holding the door shut,' said Idris, picking it up from the floor.

'Is that all you've got to secure that animal?' demanded the law.

'It's always been enough up until now,' replied Idris.

'I would advise you to put a lock on the door. Otherwise I could have you for negligence.' The constable's pride had been hurt.

On the way back, he left us as we moved into Hillside Avenue.

'Don't forget what I've told you,' warned P.C. Davies.

'OK, Will. I'll get a lock tomorrow.'

As soon as the constable had gone out of earshot, Idris said, 'No wonder they call 'im Will Book and Pencil. He'll be up there tomorrow night to see if I've put a lock on the door. If I haven't, out will come the book and pencil.'

'I think I'd better go straight back to my digs,' I said. 'This is the second wetting I've had in two days. I'm beginning to think I'm more of a Baptist minister than a Curate.'

'Be ready at half-past ten,' instructed the Vicar. 'I've arranged for Mervyn Williams to pick you up in my car to take you to St Illtyd's. And I've asked him to give you lessons in driving.'

This bombshell was delivered in the vestry two minutes before the early morning service. The prospect of a two-mile walk to the little country church had clouded my mind since getting up that morning.

'There you are,' commented Mrs Richards at breakfast when I told her of the arrangement. 'The Vicar's not such a bad old brick after all.'

'Do you know Mervyn Williams?' I asked.

'Yes, he's the boy at the garage. He's the youngest of five and all the others are in the Forces. It will be his turn to join before long. There's one thing, though, he won't have to fight those Nasties. I expect some of his brothers will be back home before he goes.'

At ten-thirty a.m. there was no sign of Mervyn. The minutes ticked by. I stood on the doorstep, clutching the case containing my robes. By ten-fifty I was beginning to panic. The service was due to start at eleven. 'Perhaps the Vicar has done something to the car after tinkering with it yesterday,' I said to Mrs Richards.

'I wouldn't think so,' replied the old lady. 'He's quite a good mechanical.'

Suddenly there was a roar of an engine down the street and Mervyn pulled up with a screeching of brakes, worthy of a gangster film.

A pale-faced young man leapt out of the car and had my case out of my hand before I could reach the pavement.

'Sorry I'm late,' he said, 'I overslept.'

'You can certainly sleep late in your house,' I replied.

'We're used to a Sunday lay in, that's the trouble.' He was like a valley edition of Sam Weller. Perky and unruffled.

In no time we were racing out of Pontywen and into the countryside. I prayed that we would meet nothing on the narrow country road – a stray cow or a frightened cyclist. We were going at such a speed that I would have been through the windscreen if he jammed his brakes on. Fortunately the coast was clear.

We arrived at St Illtyd's at ten fifty-five. I ran up the church path, flung open the church door and collided with a wall. It was six feet three in its clod-hoppers, twice my weight and smelling of strong tobacco. I disentangled my eyebrow from his top waistcoat button and looked up into the rosy full-moon of an inscrutable face.

'Where's the fire?' drawled the agricultural voice.

'Sorry,' I said, 'I thought I might be late for the service.'

'Nobody here yet,' he said drily. 'No organist, no nothing.'

'Pointless me hurrying,' I remarked, rubbing my injured ribs. 'I'm the new Curate.'

'Can see that,' replied the monolith. 'I'm Tom Cadwallader, Sexton.' He crushed my right hand. I winced.

'You must be descended from the Welsh princes, with a name like that,' I said flatteringly.

Flattery was wasted on him. He stared at me in silence. With his long-armed, bulky figure, he looked more like a descendant of Charles Darwin's original gorilla than a Welsh prince.

'Always come late 'ere,' he proclaimed. I did not know whether he was advising me to turn up late or describing the habits of the St Illtyd churchgoers. 'Vestry's down there,' he added, pointing to the east end of the church.

That was the end of our conversation. I went into the vestry and put on my cassock ready for service. A few minutes later, there was a clatter at the back of the church and an elderly, bespectacled female appeared wheeling a bicycle which she parked against the font. She was the organist, it transpired.

By the time the service commenced, there were seven in the rustic congregation who made up for their lack of numbers in the singing by the strength of their voices. The 'organ' was a harmonium powered by the vigorous feet of the organist who was obviously a demon pedal cyclist.

As I began my sermon, I was startled by a loud snore from the back of the church. It came from Tom Cadwallader, whose massive frame was in repose on the back pew. The snores continued throughout my oration. None of the congregation turned their heads towards the culprit. Obviously the snores were part of their normal Sunday service.

I announced the last hymn and the sound of the organ roused the sexton. He sighed a deep sigh and stretched his arms above his head. It was an intimidating sight.

As I was leaving, I said, 'I have never met a sexton before. What do you have to do?'

He looked down upon me as if I were an idiot, not to know a sexton's duties. 'Look after the church and dig the graves.' He sounded exhausted after that long sentence. I bade him 'good morning' and joined my chauffeur cum driving instructor.

'Do you want to drive back?' enquired Mervyn.

'If you don't mind, I should like to learn during the week,' I replied. 'I need to be in good shape on a Sunday.'

He giggled.

That afternoon, I was due to take Sunday School at St Padarn's. I decided to get there early after the morning's rush.

Two little boys were seated on the kerb of the cul-de-sac where the tin tabernacle was situated. The younger of the two stared at my clerical collar.

'Are you the prime minister?' he asked.

The elder lad intervened.

'Don't be so dull. Mr Churchill is the prime minister. This is the Minister – the church Minister.'

'Yes, that's right,' I said.

''Ow much to go in there?' asked the younger boy pointing at the church.

'You don't have to pay to go in there,' snorted the older one scornfully.

'That's true,' I said. 'Why don't you come in and find out?'

I discovered that they were brothers – Ben, the younger,

five years old and Matthew, the elder, eight. Their surname was Morris and they lived nearby on the housing estate.

'Go home and ask your mother if you can come. You'd better wash your face and hands, too,' I suggested.

They were back in no time, with more of a lick and a promise than a wash. They were still wearing the same scruffy jumpers and trousers. It was evidently a poor home.

There was a lack of male Sunday School teachers, so I decided to take the class of eight-to-ten year olds. Matthew was in my class, therefore, and Ben was in the kindergarten, presided over by Megan, a fifteen year-old girl of above-average intelligence; the type with a burning ambition to marry a curate.

Every fellow pupil was eyed critically by Matthew as they took their seats on the benches. One particular boy with a tie, a clean shirt and an immaculate grey flannel suit, viewed Matthew with distaste. The feeling was reciprocated.

'What's your name?' I said to the young advertisement for Persil.

'David Eynon.' His tone of voice implied that he was a cut above the others in the class.

'His father's a Captain.' The boy who volunteered this information was obviously in awe of him.

'Only in the Home Guard,' said another boy. 'My father's in Germany, he's a real soldier. He helped to beat Hitler.'

'And what's your name?' I asked him.

'Tommy Harris. I lives in the same street as 'im,' he said scornfully, pointing to the young Mr Eynon.

During the opening hymn, Matthew was silent, because he had never heard 'Loving Shepherd of Thy Sheep' before, while David sang loudly because he realised Matthew was a pagan.

The Lord's Prayer provided Matthew with a chance to shine. He had learnt that prayer in school. His voice could be heard outside the tin building as well as inside it. When the prayer was over, he looked at David Eynon as if to say 'beat that!'

It was a warm afternoon. As I sat down to begin the lesson, Matthew's presence made itself smelt. Captain Eynon's son and heir looked down his offended nose at the boy alongside him. Matthew glared back.

That Sunday, the Gospel was concerned with the story of the two blind men who were healed by Jesus. I launched into what I thought was a graphic presentation of the story.

'Jesus was walking through a village one day,' I said, 'when two men kept shouting at him, "Have mercy on us."'

'The disciples went to the two men and said, "Stop shouting, leave Jesus alone." When Jesus heard the disciples talk like that he told them to shut up. Then he asked the men, "What do you want me to do for you?"'

I paused, and then posed the most inane question any teacher could put to a class.

'What do you think was wrong with those two men?'

Tommy Harris spoke up.

'Deaf and dumb,' he suggested.

David Eynon snorted.

'How could they be deaf and dumb when they shouted?' he asked scornfully.

'Come on,' I said, 'let's have another answer.' I could see a gleam of inspiration come into Matthew's eyes.

He glanced at young Master Eynon as if to say, 'Wait for this.'

He launched himself into his triumphal answer.

'Gastro-enteritis,' he proclaimed. There was a gasp from the rest of the class, including David Eynon. They gazed in wonder at such a long word coming from so unlikely a source.

'A good try, Matthew,' I pronounced. He beamed. 'But I'm afraid,' I went on, 'that it is not right. To end any further speculation, I must tell you that they were two blind men.'

'Perhaps they had gastro-enteritis as well,' said Matthew, unwilling to surrender.

'Maybe they did,' I replied. 'Some of the food they ate in those days was not very clean. So it's quite likely they may have had gastro-enteritis.'

He looked David Eynon in the eye, as if daring him to make a comment. He need not have worried. There was none forthcoming. We reached the climax of the story without any further sign of animosity between the two boys.

Then we sang the last hymn. It was 'Lamb of God, I look to Thee, Thou would'st my example be.' The volume of noise from David Eynon singing into the silent Matthew's ear was more suited to the tap room of a pub on a Saturday night than a Sunday School.

'Bloody show-off,' snarled Matthew from the corner of his mouth, emphasising his contempt with a discreet elbow into the Eynon ribs.

The blow caught the singer right in the middle of 'Give me an obedient heart', causing a squeak to replace the bellow. An outburst of giggling from the rest of the class caused a distinct diminuendo in the singing of the whole school.

I stopped the hymn.

'What's going on here?' I demanded.

'It's his fault, sir,' spoke up the detestable Eynon. 'He swore and then hit me.'

'I didn't hit 'im, sir,' said Matthew. 'I was 'olding my book like this with my elbow out and 'e turned round to sing loud and 'it 'is ribs against my elbow.'

'Ask him if he swore, sir,' winced the stricken one.

'I only told 'im 'e was showing off,' said Matthew, 'and 'e was.'

'He said "bloody", sir,' persisted David Eynon.

'Enough of this,' I said sternly. 'Let's have the last verse and there's no need to shout. You are supposed to sing.'

Matthew preened his grubby feathers.

A few minutes later he was escorting his little brother from the building with a firm promise that he would be back next week. It must have sounded like a dire threat to the Eynon child who was standing nearby.

Outside number thirteen Mount Pleasant View, when I arrived back from Sunday School, was a large Wolsey saloon. No sooner had I opened the door, than I was met by a tall, thin, bean-pole of a man with an incongruous Billy Bunter face, half covered in huge horn-rimmed spectacles. He had a college scarf wound round his neck.

'Fred!' he squeaked. 'Found you.'

Harry Tench was a college acquaintance of stunted intelligence but blessed with a rich doctor as a father. It was only through influence combined with mercy that he struggled to accomplish in five years what ordinary mortals achieved in three.

The last time I'd seen him, a year ago, was during the degree examinations. I called to see him in his digs over a grocer's shop. He wished to borrow a book from me. His landlady ushered me into his presence. I shall never forget the sight. He was ensconced in his armchair, with a wet towel around his head and his feet in a bowl of water, staring at his books with owlish incomprehension.

'What on earth are you doing?' I asked.

'You should try it,' he replied. 'It keeps your head cool and the cold water on your feet will keep you awake till the early hours of the morning. This way is much better than black coffee for that.'

'I'll stick to black coffee,' I said.

It would have been wiser for him to have done the same. Later that week the constant immersion of his feet in a bowl of water had a gradual effect upon his bladder. So it was that about two o'clock in the morning, Harry had an overwhelming desire to empty the said bladder. The bathroom was on the first floor which meant a journey downstairs from the attic, otherwise known as the second floor, where the student was marooned.

To make the journey would require several seconds which Harry could not spare. To a man of action, such as himself, the solution was simple: open the window and empty the bladder. A heavy shower descended from the second floor. What Harry had forgotten was the corrugated iron roof over the stock-room below. The peace of the June early morning was shattered by what sounded like bursts of heavy machine-gun fire. Frightened neighbours opened windows, fearing the worst, while Mrs Thomas, the grocer's wife, opened the window immediately below to catch the last drops from above.

He failed the examinations and was given a warning from the College Board about his irresponsible conduct. Now here he was in my digs in Pontywen and obviously excited. He always squeaked when he was excited.

'I've passed,' he exclaimed in top soprano. 'So I've brought back the book you lent me.'

'How did you find me here?' I asked.

'That was easy,' he said. 'Somebody told me you were in Pontywen. I just went to the Vicarage and got your address.'

'But that car – whose is that and how have you got petrol coupons?'

'The car is my father's and he gets coupons because he is a doctor. He had a lift to the golf club, so I've pinched it for a few hours. Thought you might like a run in it – an escape from this hole.'

'It's not a hole, but I wouldn't mind a ride. As long as I'm back by five o'clock. I'm preaching tonight at the parish church.'

'I've got to be back by six at the latest, before the old man gets back from the golf club.'

Harry's foot was as hard on the accelerator as Mervyn's had been in the morning. Surprised spectators in the streets of Pontywen must have thought we were the leaders in the first Pontywen road-race.

'Do you think you could slow down a little? I know I have to be back by five but I want to be back in one piece.'

My remonstration had the desired effect.

'Sorry old man,' he said, blinking through his spectacles. 'I get carried away by the sheer power of the machine.'

'If you're not careful, you'll get carried away by an ambulance,' I warned.

We sailed along the roads gently, up into the hills. It was a lovely afternoon. We parked on a hill top. The moorland stretched for miles around. Not a soul was in sight. The only sound came from hovering skylarks – and from Harry who was in reminiscent mood.

'I'm afraid I got drunk celebrating my degree,' he said. 'I had a hell of a row from my landlady. On the way up here, I was thinking about the time when you got drunk and your landlady threw you out.'

'She didn't exactly throw me out, Harry,' I replied. 'She just made sure I didn't come back to her next term.'

That incident happened towards the end of my first term in college. Mrs Evans, my landlady, was a parsimonious body who economised on food, fuel and light. She counted the grains of sugar in the bowl. There was more heat in an Eskimo's front parlour than there was in my front room. No lamp she ever used was over forty watts in strength so that, whenever I studied, my face was so close to my books that the end of my nose was always anointed with printer's ink.

Then there was her dog, a yapping, stinky, mouse-coloured, mouse-sized pekinese called Jinny. Its coat was continually shedding hairs, not only on the carpet but also on the armchair in my room where it used to rest. What is more, it not only yapped, but it also bit me whenever I tried to remove it forcibly from my chair.

To add to this catalogue of misery, there was the key. Mrs Evans had only one key to her residence and it never left her possession. I think she must have slept with it under her pillow, where it kept her false teeth company. Anyway, this hard fact of life meant that I had to be back in my digs before she went to bed – and that was about nine o'clock.

The end of my first term was drawing near, like the end of my tether.

I was supposed to stay with Mrs Evans for another two terms. The prospect was daunting. However, there was the exciting thought of the Christmas dinner arranged for honours students in my year. Since the function was not scheduled to begin until eight p.m., either Mrs Evans would have to forego part of her beauty sleep or she would have to surrender the key for that night.

The problem was resolved on the morning of the dinner. 'You can have the key tonight, bach,' she said. 'Don't make a noise coming in and don't lose the key, it's the only one I've got.' As if I didn't know.

A good time was had by all at the dinner. I had never drunk so much wine in my young life. Then, to cap it all, my friend, Don, managed to 'scrounge' an unopened bottle after the proceedings and invited me to his digs to empty it between us. His landlady's place was next-door-but-one to mine, the intervening door belonging to Bethesda Chapel.

We drank the wine in teacups, the drinking interspersed with maudlin conversation which became increasingly incoherent. I do remember dimly, Don, drunkenly trying to sober me with the following words; 'If you're not careful, you're going to wake up in the morning and find yourself asleep in Bethesda's pulpit.' He made several attempts at 'Bethesda' before getting the word out.

At one a.m. we whispered an hysterical farewell on his doorstep. It was the time of the blackout, but at least it was a moonlit night. I had to walk a full fifty yards past the chapel to number one Bethesda Terrace.

I decided that my plan of campaign was to find the white line in the middle of the road and follow it if I could. Then, having reached my digs, I would go at right angles to my front door. I staggered my way down the road, deviating from the line frequently. When I reached the middle of the road outside my digs, I decided to make straight for the front door.

Instead, I hit the front window with considerable force. Next I slid to the door and spent an eternity trying to get that key into the lock. The dog started to yap, then the window upstairs opened and a toothless hag hissed at me, 'Keep quiet, you'll wake up the neighbourhood.'

Lights came on in the bedrooms of numbers two, three and four. They must have thought the Germans had landed. At the last, the Lord delivered me out of my panic. The twentieth effort to fit the key to the lock succeeded.

Once I got into my room, I was faced with the dilemma of the key – where to leave it. First I tried in my room, then the table in my landlady's room. I came to the conclusion that it did not look right up there, so I took it back to my room. After surveying the key, now reposed on a copy of the Shorter Oxford English Dictionary, I thought it best to leave it.

Getting into bed was an ordeal. The bed would not stay still long enough for me to get into it. At last I succeeded in holding it down and collapsed on top of the bedclothes.

That was when the moon-beams decided to attack me. They were coming in between a gap in the curtains. Whenever I opened my eyes, they kept firing at me, alternately at my right eye, then at my left.

The moment had come for a counter attack from myself. I fell out of bed, picked myself up and launched my body at the curtains to shut out the marauders. I pulled so hard at the material that the shaky old rail came out of its holders and fell on me, trapping me in a prison of chintz.

Jinny started to yap. The next second, my bedroom door was flung open and from inside the curtains I heard a distant voice. It said, 'That's it. I've had enough of you. You're not coming back next term.' Drunk though I was, I realised they were the nicest words she had ever spoken to me.

'At least I can tell you that now I have a landlady who is a peach. She is more of a Mrs Malaprop than anybody I have ever met – but she feeds me well and looks after me well.'

I looked at my watch. 'It's half past four, Harry,' I said. 'We ought to be getting back.'

'Hop in, friend,' he invited jauntily.

I hopped in. He clambered into the driver's seat and turned the ignition key. Nothing happened. He tried again, to no avail. Then he tried several times in quick succession, swearing at the car with ever-increasing vehemence. The engine remained unmoved.

'Do you know anything about cars?' he asked in desperation.

'You're joking,' I said. 'More important – do you?'

'All I know is how to start it and stop it.'

'In that case, you had better start it,' I suggested.

'That's not funny,' he snarled.

The road over the moors stretched into infinity, devoid of any sign of human life.

A nightmare vision of Canon Llewellyn, in his robes, surrounded by the choir, fuming as he waited for the Curate, flashed upon my inward eye.

'For heaven's sake, do something. Get the bonnet up and fiddle around with the wires and things,' I urged him.

'A brilliant suggestion, Secombe,' he snorted.

'If I don't get back soon, I'll be getting the boot from the Vicar.'

'And if I don't get back, my old man will kill me.'

'Enough of this badinage. Get that bonnet up,' I ordered.

'I don't know how to get the bonnet up,' he confessed.

'You're as bad as I am,' I replied ruefully.

After fiddling around in front of the car, he managed to raise the bonnet. We both stood, staring at the mechanical wonders now revealed to us.

'Go on then,' I said, 'see if you can find something loose or something that's come apart.'

'Look at it,' he squeaked. 'Everything's covered in grease. This is an expensive suit I've got on. I'm not going to mess that up for you or anybody else. I've got some muck on my fingers already through opening that bonnet.'

He took a handkerchief from his top pocket and tried to remove the grease from his hands.

Harry always was a dandy. He would parade the streets with the college scarf wound around his neck and carrying a rolled umbrella. Summer or winter, rain or shine, the umbrella remained rolled. It was rumoured that it was really a walking-stick with cloth for camouflage.

'I'm not standing here doing nothing. I'm going to start walking back to Pontywen.' Angrily I stepped out along the road.

'It must be ten miles away.' His voice coming from behind me had now reached top soprano and had a large number of decibels. I ignored him.

As I went, I cursed the man who had invented the combustion engine. That invention had caused me more than enough trouble in the past week. The incessant song of the skylarks, which had enchanted me half an hour ago, became a nasty irritant.

'Shut up,' I shouted – but the birds took no notice.

I was sticky with sweat and out of breath after walking for a couple of miles at an olympic pace. Not a house, not a soul was in sight. There must have been more comings and goings in the Sahara than there were on this road. I looked at my watch. It was half past five. In an hour's time, the service was due to start. My legs were already beginning to buckle.

Then in the far distance, I thought I could see some kind of vehicle coming towards me. I was in such a state of mind, that I thought it might be a mirage. However the mirage could now be heard.

It was an Army truck. I stood in the middle of the road and, with arms outstretched, waited for it to reach me.

A somewhat surprised corporal jumped down from his seat.

'What's the matter, padre?' he asked anxiously.

'It's my friend's car. It's broken down, back up the road. I've got to get to Pontywen for a service at half past six,' I said between pants.

'Get in, padre. We'll see what we can do.' He sounded the kind of man who would know what to do.

By the time we reached the car, Harry Tench was in the

extreme stages of hysteria, his voice reaching stratospheric levels.

'I tried to do something with the wires and things. The car's still not going. But look at my suit!' There were patches of grease on the jacket of his expensive light-grey suit.

'Calm down, Harry. Our friend here will see what he can do to get the car started. Perhaps Mrs Richards can do something about your jacket.'

'Let's see what's wrong,' said the corporal.

After a couple of seconds of examination of the machine's anatomy, his diagnosis was a loose connection. The use of a spanner produced an instant cure. He pressed his foot on the accelerator and revelled in the roar which resulted.

'Lovely engine,' he pronounced.

'All I know,' I said, 'is that it's a lovely sound after the deathly hush.'

By now, Harry had recovered his composure and thanked the soldier in baritone tones, instead of falsetto.

It was six o'clock when we drew up outside thirteen Mount Pleasant View.

'Come on in and let Mrs Richards see what she can do about the suit,' I suggested.

'No, thank you, Fred,' he replied. 'I want to get back before my father, if possible.'

I arrived in the vestry with a minute to spare. The Vicar glowered at me.

'What time do you call this?' he snapped.

'My apologies,' I said as I struggled into my robes. 'A college friend arrived unexpectedly this afternoon.'

'An odd kind of friend to disturb your Sunday,' commented my superior.

'He's certainly odd,' I agreed.

6

It was a miserable morning. The rain was incessant, stair rods of water alternating with mist. Thick valley mist.

As I made my way to the Vicarage, the rain cascading from my umbrella, Bertie Owen was coming down the street on the opposite side, raincoat buttoned up around his neck and a sodden trilby on his head.

'Terrible weather,' I shouted.

'It certainly is,' he replied, wiping a raindrop from the end of his nose.

'Like the Flood,' I commented.

He stopped in his tracks.

'What flood, Mr Secombe?'

'You know,' I said. 'Noah and the Ark, stuck on Mount Ararat.'

'Haven't read the papers for days,' he bawled. 'See you Sunday.'

I was still chuckling when I rang the Vicarage doorbell. The chuckle disappeared when the Vicar opened the door. Obviously it was not one of his better mornings. His face was in tune with the weather.

Once behind his desk in the study, he launched into a critique of my Sunday evening sermon which he considered to be shallow.

'You need more bottom, Secombe,' he declared. 'More bottom.'

That's what my mother always says, I thought: no bottom, straight as a board, back and front, not a curve in sight.

'You need to see more of human misery. It's time you visited the workhouse,' he grunted.

My eyebrows shot up.

'I go there occasionally to give some pastoral care,' he went on. 'Perhaps you would like to take on that duty. It will be an education for you.'

The Vicar permitted himself a small grimace, intended as a smile.

'When do I start, Canon?' I asked.

'No time like the present,' he said. 'Go this afternoon and introduce yourself to Mr Wolstenholme, the Master. He's a Yorkshireman, plain spoken. But I think he has the interests of the inmates at heart. His wife, Matron, is a difficult character.'

When I told Mrs Richards that I had been given the position of clerical visitor to the workhouse, she was most sympathetic.

'Mr Price was given that job by the Vicar,' she said. 'But he'd been here a lot longer than you when that happened. He didn't like it one bit. He couldn't get on with that Mr what-you-call, the Master. Worse still with Mrs what-you-call. Not only that, he couldn't stand the smell of those intakes. He said it was high in the heaven.'

'Did he indeed?' I said. 'If the smell is as high as that, it must be bad.'

By the time I set out for my visit the sun had made its appearance and it was very warm. Already I could sense the assault on my nostrils in the workhouse.

Unlike the hospital, which was perched on the hillside, Pontywen Lodge was closeted in the Valley. Just outside the town. It was surrounded by large stone walls, giving the impression from the outside of a prison. Inside the walls that impression remained. The dirty brown stone of the building was inset with a large quota of small, barred windows. There was one redeeming feature – the 'drive' was bordered by a number of rhododendron trees competing for space and encroaching on the tarmac. Pot-holes riddled the surface of the drive which, like the pools mentioned in one of the psalms, were filled with water.

The entrance to the workhouse was worthy of that most forbidding of inscriptions, 'Abandon hope all ye who enter here.' However, it did possess a large push-button doorbell which, when I pushed it, echoed as loudly as St Matthias' Church bell.

An elderly female in drab workhouse garb appeared, her small wizened face surmounted by a few straggling grey hairs on an otherwise bald head. She stared at my clerical collar. Before she could speak, the unmistakable accent of Yorkshire bellowed in the background, 'It's all reet, Nellie. I'll see to t'Reverend.'

The dapper gentleman in his neat grey pinstripe suit who clattered over the stone floor to greet me was more like a commercial traveller than a workhouse master.

'Name's Wally Wolstenholme. You must be t'new Curate. I wondered when I'd be seeing you.' He thrust out his right hand and clamped mine in its vice-like grip.

'Pleased to meet you, Mr Wolstenholme,' I said. 'The Vicar asked me to call and spend an hour or so this afternoon, so here I am.'

As I spoke, he peered at me through his thick pebbled spectacles and swirled his dentures around the inside of his mouth. It was very disconcerting. I was concerned lest they would not be in place by the next time he spoke. I need not have worried.

'Well,' he said, with teeth back in position immediately, 'Let's take you on tour of this grand institution. Any time you want a holiday, you know where to come.'

'Thank you,' I replied, 'but I prefer the seaside.'

'Glad to see you've got a sense of humour, lad.' He stopped at a door marked 'Matron'. 'Your predecessor, Price, were gormless, if you'll excuse me saying so. I'll say nowt more about that. Now then, you must meet t'other half of t'firm.'

The Master knocked on the door and waited for an answer.

'Come in!' barked a female voice.

I was ushered into the presence of a small lady, looking every inch a hospital matron, in her head dress and her starched linen.

'Matron,' said the master, 'this is t' new Curate.'

She rose from behind her desk. Like my Vicar she found it difficult to smile. Like the Vicar, too, she had gimlet eyes which bored into you – except her eyes had two centres like hard black coal.

'Good afternoon, matron.' I spoke in tones of due deference.

She made no attempt to come to meet me and shake my hand.

'Well, Wally, what is t'gentleman's name?' she demanded.

'It's Secombe,' I said, not waiting for her husband. 'Fred Secombe.'

Still staying behind her desk, she said, 'Pleased to meet you, Mr Secombe.' Then she sat down with an air of finality.

'If you'll excuse me,' she went on, 'I have a lot to do. The Master will show you around, I'm sure.'

'She's got a lot to do at t'moment,' explained the Master, as if to excuse his wife's abrupt manner. 'Short staffed and overworked.'

He led me down the corridor which badly needed the application of a paint brush. As he walked with his hands in his pockets, he demonstrated another of his accomplishments, the swirling around of coins in his pocket, in synchronisation with the swirling around of the dentures in his mouth.

'We turn left here,' he directed. Just off the corridor was the entrance to a ward. He knocked and entered without waiting for a reply. As he opened the door, the stench of urine rushed out to greet me.

'Sorry about t'smell,' he said. 'This is where we have t'bed-ridden males. Incontinent most of 'em. Fast as you change t'bed, they've peed in it again.'

There were a dozen beds occupied by slumbering forms, dozing in the fug of the warm afternoon. No nurse was visible.

'I expect Nurse Jones has had to pop out,' he explained. 'It's best to come and talk to poor buggers in t'morning.'

The silence was as depressing as the smell. Here were twelve old men queueing up to die. The only time they would leave that ward would be to visit the mortuary.

'Yes, I'll do that,' I said turning to go out again. It was becoming obvious why the Vicar thought that visits to the workhouse would broaden my education.

'Let's go and see t'females across the way,' said the

Master. 'Smell is not quite so bad and some of 'em will be awake at least.'

We crossed the corridor and once again the Master knocked on the door. A soprano voice shrilled. 'Wait a minute.' This was followed by the screaming of an elderly harridan.

'That's Mary Ann,' commented the Master. 'I often say she should be in a strait jacket in an asylum. The only one to handle her is Matron.'

I could imagine that one look from those penetrating eyes would be enough to calm the most recalcitrant of inmates.

We waited a while, as the Master amused himself with his teeth and his coins.

Suddenly he broke the silence. 'Secombe,' he mused. 'That's not a Welsh name, is it?'

'No, it's a Cornish name. My great-grandfather was a sailor who married a Swansea woman and then settled in Swansea.' Then I added, 'Just like you and Mrs Wolstenholme, obviously Yorkshire folk, are in Pontywen.'

His face reddened. I had touched him on a raw spot.

'Nay, lad,' he said firmly. 'We aren't in Pontywen to stay. We've been here eight or nine years and we're ready to go now t'war's over. Things are going to change. Workhouses are on t'way out, believe me. We'll be back up North, ere long, I expect, perhaps in administrative jobs with old people or summat.'

His prognostications were cut short by the opening of the door of the female ward. An auburn-haired, red-faced, young nurse found herself confronted by the Master and the Curate.

'Sorry to keep you waiting, both,' she said. 'It was Mary Ann. You know what she's like, Master.'

'Only too well,' he replied.

'I had to get Nurse Jones to help me get her back into bed. She's been terrible, upsetting the whole ward, as usual. Anyway she's all right now, for the time being.'

We moved into the ward. Nurse Jones, a grey-haired, middle-aged lady, was on her way out.

'Have you been in my ward, Master?' she asked. 'Sorry I had to leave it but they were all asleep when I left.'

'They still are, nurse,' he said. 'And will be for some time by the look of them.'

Most of the elderly females were sitting up. Some of them simply clutching at the blankets and staring into space. Two of them were talking to themselves in an undistinguishable babble. In the corner bed, close to the door, was the troublemaker, sitting bolt upright and staring at me.

'Who's he?' she asked. 'What's he doing here?'

'Now then, Mary Ann,' said the Master. 'This is Mr Secombe, the new Curate of the church.'

'Come here, love,' she demanded.

I went to her bedside. She seized my hand and held on to it, moving it back and forth. With her wild eyes, her unkempt white hair and her toothless mouth, she was perfectly suited for the role of one of the Witches in *Macbeth*.

'I'm very religious, I am,' she confided. 'I know my Bible, I do.'

The next minute, she dropped my hand and stood upon the bed. Off came her nightgown to reveal her desiccated body. 'Naked came I into this world,' she intoned.

Before she could say any more, the nurse and the Master had covered her in her bedclothes. In the meantime I had made a quick exit.

Some minutes later, Wally Wolstenholme emerged, looking somewhat flustered.

'I must apologise for that,' he said. 'You never know what she's going to do next.'

'It was quite an experience, I must admit,' I replied. 'She was hardly a Mae West, was she?'

'Day rooms next,' suggested the Master. 'One for the men, one for the women. We'll have a look at the women's room for a minute and then I'll leave you with the men.'

In the women's day room there were about twenty old ladies. Some sitting in the wooden armchairs which lined the walls while a few were wandering aimlessly in and out of the open door into the sunshine. A faint smell of stale urine hung in the air.

'This is where your caravan had better rest for today,' announced the master as he showed me into the men's day room. A strong smell of pipe tobacco, 'Diggers Shag' type, filled the room. There was a table in the centre at which sat a bearded patriarch, obviously a vagrant. He was engrossed in what appeared to be a tattered old encyclopaedia.

'Our only Casual at the moment,' I was told. The rest of the men in the room sat in their armchairs around the room, a few smoking pipes, and all of them staring quietly into space. It was a terrifying picture of old age.

The Master left me to get back to his duties after telling me I would be welcome any time.

I decided to join the old tramp at the table.

'Reading anything interesting?' I asked.

He looked up from his studies.

'Let me put it this way, Father,' he said. 'I'm like a mountain sheep hoping to pick up scraps of useful information.' The voice was cultured.

'I don't wish to be impertinent,' I replied, 'but why is a person of your obvious intelligence in a place like this.'

His faded blue eyes focussed on me.

'You have much to learn about life, my son,' he said. 'I wore a collar like yours once.'

I gasped.

'Don't be shocked, I am not the only priest who has ended on the scrap heap. There are many roads which can lead to it. The route I took was directed by the bottle, which at first was a friend and then became a master.'

'My apologies for the impertinence, Father,' I said.

'No need to apologise,' he replied. 'It was a natural question to ask me. The only other information I will give you is that I am an Oxford man like your Vicar and that I was Vicar of St John's.' He mentioned a parish in South Wales. 'If I am still here on Sunday, I shall be at your early-morning Mass. Very few to see the old reprobate at that service.'

He stood and shook my hand. A man of at least six foot in height, he was an impressive figure as he towered over me.

'The Lord be with you,' he said quietly. Then he sat down. 'And now, if you don't mind, I shall continue with my studies.'

As I reached the door, he looked up and said, 'Remember me when you come into your kingdom.' Those words have haunted me ever since.

It was a long walk back home. Every step plunged me

further into gloom, as I contemplated the depths of human misery, from the deathbed queues of the 'bed-bound' to the tragedy of the alcoholic priest.

By the time I reached my 'digs' I was in a state of deep depression.

'I thought you'd be like this,' was Mrs Richards' greeting. 'Mr Price used to be the same. He'd go to the pictures to forget all about it.'

'Perhaps I ought to do that,' I said, 'or something like it.'

'Well,' replied my landlady, 'I've got a ticket for those "Cong." concert people. If you'd like to go, you can have it. It's imperial to me whether I go or not. I've seen them before.'

The Congregationalist Minister was a young man with an interest in theatricals. He had formed a concert party from the ladies in his church. Most of them had seen their fiftieth birthday long ago. One of them, Mrs Simons, lived in our street. She was a peroxide blonde whose hair should have been grey long before the War. She was the soubrette, according to what she told me once. 'You must come and see us,' she had burbled.

'If she's the soubrette,' I said to myself, 'it must be worth going.'

Pontywen Congregational Church Hall was filled to its capacity of a hundred and fifty for the latest performance of the Valley 'Fol-de-Rols', as they called themselves. Molly Williams, the daughter from the Post Office, was presiding at the piano. She was a likeable young lady who was handicapped in her speech by a cleft palate.

On my entry into the hall I was recognised as the Curate of the parish church. Accordingly I was given a place of honour in the front row among a number of deacons and their wives. From their conversation, they seemed more apprehensive than enthusiastic about the entertainment.

'I hear he's got some very sarcastic things to say in a song about the Beveridge Report,' said a red-faced gentleman. 'Next minute he'll be criticising the Labour party. You can't be 'aving politics from a minister.'

'Not only that,' added a lady, 'some of these costumes the women are wearing are really a bit . . . you know.'

There were grunts of approval for these remarks from the

others in the front row. An interesting evening was in prospect.

The first item on the programme was described as 'Tally-ho' performed by the ensemble. The 'ensemble' was composed of eight mature ladies, dressed in hunting jackets in various shades of pink and red, over very short skirts revealing various degrees of bulging female flesh. Their top-hats were made of cardboard, painted black.

Each held a stick in front of her which represented a riding whip. This was held with two arms outstretched by six of the performers and with two arms half-stretched by two ladies at the back. The intention was to indicate horse riding.

'A hunting we will go,' they sang, with off key vigour, their vocal efforts as rugged as their terpsichorean exhibition. The choreography consisted of two steps forward, followed by two steps backward, repeated *ad nauseam* throughout the item.

There was one variation to this routine. This was when they moved into a rendition of 'Run, Rabbit, Run'. At the mention of 'the farmer's gun', six of them raised the stick to their shoulders while the two ladies at the back continued to ride their horses. Evidently the latter were of the opinion that rabbits were not chased by people on horseback.

The curtains closed to generous applause from relatives and friends of the performers and to as much clapping from the rest of the audience as in the members' enclosure at Lord's during a university match.

Then followed a contralto solo 'Art thou troubled?' which must have been addressed to Molly Williams at the piano who found great difficulty with Handel's music. A recitation by Madame Rees-Morris who had qualifications after her name was next. Entitled 'The Single Hair', it described the devotion of a bald-headed man to the last surviving evidence of a once hirsute condition. Then one day it fell into his soup at a restaurant. He retrieved it, dried it and put it in his wallet. Then he took it to a taxidermist and had it stuffed. This was delivered as if it were a soliloquy from *Hamlet*. There was no laughter but tremendous appreciation at the conclusion for the excellent elocution which had been demonstrated.

Next on the programme was 'Selected item by Adeline

Simons'. 'So that's her name,' I thought, 'Sweet Adeline.' The curtains opened to reveal Mrs Simons with a blue bow in her peroxide and with an Alice Blue gown. 'It has to be,' I said to myself, ' "In my quaint little Alice Blue gown".' I was wrong.

She smiled coyly at the audience and nodded at Molly at the piano. From the first note it was obvious that something was wrong. 'Daddy wouldn't buy me . . .' she sang. Molly was playing something which sounded like grand opera. The discord continued for some seconds and ended in dead silence.

Mrs Simons came forward to the edge of the platform. 'What are you playing, Molly?' she demanded.

'I'm playing "My Hero" from *The Chocolate Soldier*,' said Molly in aggrieved tones.

'That's not what we agreed on,' proclaimed Mrs Simons in high dudgeon. 'I distinctly said "Daddy wouldn't buy me a bow-wow" first and then "My Hero".'

'I'm sorry, Addie,' replied Molly, 'But that's what you said, I'm positive.'

'So am I positive,' shouted Mrs Simons.

The audience was hushed and intent, with heads going to and fro watching the protagonists, like the crowd at Wimbledon. It must have been the most attentive audience the 'Fol-de-Rols' had ever had.

'Right,' said the soubrette, 'Let's begin with "Daddy wouldn't buy me a bow-wow".'

'If you say so,' came the voice from the piano.

'I do say so,' replied Addie with a stamp of her foot.

She turned away from the pianist and addressed the audience.

By a great effort of self control she transformed her facial appearance from a snarl to a sickly smile.

'For my first song,' she announced, 'I shall sing "Daddy wouldn't buy me a bow-wow".'

To the accompaniment of a scowling Molly, she embarked upon a simpering version of the Music Hall ditty.

When the song ended in complete silence, she curtseyed and said, 'Thank you! For my encore I give you "My Hero" from *The Chocolate Soldier*.'

From the reaction of the audience, it appeared that no one was prepared to accept the donation.

Dauntless, Adeline Simons launched into a tuneless rendition which quailed at every top note. Even her relatives, if any were present, would not have dared to cheer. As her last note died suddenly through lack of breath, the curtains came across quickly to prevent any further embarrassment.

Relentlessly the programme continued. The little minister provided his *pièce de résistance*, words and music written by himself. Quite witty and musically pleasing, it was much the best item in the concert. He must have been the star performer in his College dramatics. However, he was suffering from an attempt to make bricks without straw with the material provided by his congregation.

The penultimate item in the second half of the programme was billed as 'The Burglars', a sketch, by Adeline Simons and Gwen Jones. There was a lull preceding the sketch while preparations were made to set the scene. Eventually the curtains opened jerkily to reveal what was intended to be the inside of a bank. Two borrowed wardrobes covered in grey paper represented two large safes.

Enter the two burglars dressed in Pontywen's black and white striped rugby jerseys and trousers borrowed from the respective husbands. On their heads were caps, obtained from the same source. Each carried a torch, which was quite unnecessary, since the footlights and the floodlights were at full strength. As Adeline Simons turned to Gwen Jones to speak her first line, 'Which safe shall we do first?', it became manifest to the audience that the flies of her trousers were undone. An expanse of red bloomers was revealed. At first a titter, followed by full-bodied laughter rocked the assembled throng, with the exception of the deacons in the front row.

Adeline and Gwen had never had such appreciation of their talents. Their faces shone with pleasure.

'Eeny-meeny-miney-mo,' intoned Gwen, pointing at the safes alternately. Then suddenly she pointed at the expanse of red bloomers.

'Ooh!' she screamed from a bending position.

'Ahh!' screeched Adeline as she looked down, covering the gap with her two hands, like a full-back facing a free kick in the goal area.

The screams gave place to embarrassed laughter from the two performers as they fell about the stage.

'Curtains!' shouted the Minister from the side. The curtains came across with such force that they almost shot off the runners.

It was at this stage that I 'made an excuse and left', to use the immortal phrase of investigators employed by Sunday newspapers. My ribs had taken such a hammering that they were in danger of breaking.

When Mrs Richards opened the door to me, she said, 'Well, Mr Secombe, you're a sight for bad eyes, laughing all over the place.'

'Thank you very much for the ticket,' I replied. 'It was worth every penny you paid for it.'

'I didn't pay anything. It was a compliment one from Mrs Simons,' explained my landlady.

'What ever it was, I'm most grateful,' I said. 'In fact it's given me the urge to introduce Gilbert and Sullivan to Pontywen.'

She looked puzzled. 'What gentlemen are they?' she asked.

7

I was sitting in the back yard on a dining-chair, borrowed by permission of my landlady. It was a lovely morning for a sun-bathe. To this end I had covered my nose with the top right-hand corner of the front page of *The Times* which I had glued to my skin with saliva.

With my face turned towards the sun, I began to compile an imaginary entry for the 'Handy Hints' section of the church magazine insert which was published nationally. Last month's five-shilling prize had been awarded to a lady who advocated the use of empty perfume bottles to 'sweeten your drawers'.

I contemplated the wording of my entry. 'Here is a useful tip for proboscis protection in hot sunshine. Take the top right hand corner of the front page of *The Times*. Carefully cut the paper to match the size of your nose. Apply saliva to the paper and press it with three fingers, holding the protective shield in position for thirty seconds.'

Suddenly my reverie was interrupted by the noisy emergence of the three little boys who lived next door. They were Daniel (Danny), aged eight; Llewellyn (Lew), aged seven and Leonard (Lennie), aged four.

'For God's sake get out from under my feet,' shouted their mother, Mrs Preece. Her husband was an air gunner in the Air Force, stationed in India. Looking after three lively lads during the school holidays was proving a trial for her.

Each back yard in the Street was separated from the others by a five-foot stone wall, composed of irregular pieces of quarried stone, interspersed with wild flowers which had invaded the cement.

From behind the wall I could hear a theological discussion

developing. The boys had been sent to the nearest Sunday School by their mother who gained an hour or so's oasis of peace thereby. As that Sunday School was held in the wooden Pentecostal Church at the end of the Street, the boys had been instructed about the dangers of blasphemy.

'She shouldn't take God's name in vain,' said Danny, the eldest. He was a bright lad.

'He could strike her dead,' was Lew's comment.

'Yes,' replied Danny. 'He's all-powerful. He's made everything – the sun and the moon and the stars.'

'And he made this world,' said Lew, 'the trees, the flowers and the fields.'

A competition now ensued between the two boys to claim the most of God's achievements. Eventually mental exhaustion set in and there was silence as they searched in their minds for something else God had made.

Suddenly there was a contribution from Lennie the four-year-old.

'It's the Council made the houses, though.'

'Shut up you, Lenny,' retorted Danny. 'You don't know what we are talking about.'

Not long after this, I fell asleep.

The next thing I knew there was a loud shattering of glass behind me.

Nestling along the back wall was a memorial to the late Mr Richards. He had been a keen gardener. Apparently Pontywen Station had been given the accolade of the station with the best kept flowerbeds on the line on two occasions when he was in charge.

At home his pride and joy was the little greenhouse in his back yard. Every year it produced tomatoes and cucumbers in abundance. After his death, Mrs Richards kept the glass in spotless condition, cleaning it every week. Nothing grew in it. There were just the fossilised stalks, the widow's permanent mementoes of her husband's hobby.

'How many times have I told you not to play ball in the back yard?' screeched Mrs Preece.

'It was Lennie's fault,' said Danny. 'Lew and me was playing quietly with the cricket ball and he came and took the ball and threw it over the wall.'

'You shouldn't have had the ball in the first place,' shouted his mother. 'Now you've done something to Mr Richards' greenhouse.' It was still 'Mr Richards' Greenhouse'.

I stood up and surveyed the damage. Two large panes of glass were in smithereens.

'Sorry about this, Mr Secombe.' The embarrassed face of Mrs Preece appeared over the wall. 'Is it very much? I'll pay for the damage.'

'It's only two panes,' I said. 'Mrs Richards is out shopping at the moment. Hold on, I'll get the ball for the boys.'

'I think you had better keep it – for the time being anyway. It's much too hard for little boys to be playing with. Their father gave it to Danny before he went out to India four years ago. My husband was Captain of Pontywen Cricket Club, you see.' She said this with an air of pride.

'He must be a good cricketer,' I replied. 'I used to play for the College seconds and once or twice for the firsts. Anyway, now that the War is over, I don't suppose it will be very long before he'll be back to captain Pontywen.'

'They say it will be at least six months before he's back,' she said, with a sigh. 'It can't be soon enough for me nor for the boys. Danny and Lew worship him. Lennie was born just after he'd gone but he's longing to see his dad.'

'I'll tell you what, Mrs Preece,' I replied. 'It's my day off today. I have a bat which I brought to swank with in my college days. The boys have a ball. So we could join up for a game on the Welfare ground this afternoon.'

Her face lit up.

'That's very kind of you, Mr Secombe,' she said. 'The boys will be thrilled.'

'Tell them, I'll call for them at half past two. I'll hang on to the ball till then.'

When I went back into the house I searched in the 'cubby-hole' under the stairs to find my cricket bat which was hidden under a multitude of impedimenta. Eventually I unearthed it: a battle-scarred piece of wood which had suffered from my ill-timed strokes.

As a schoolboy I had dreams of becoming a fine cricketer like my maternal grandfather, Thomas Arthur Davies. It was his proud boast that he bowled a couple of overs against W.G.

Grace. He never said what had happened to his bowling that day. However, he did possess a yellowed cutting from a newspaper recording his feat of taking all ten wickets in an innings for just two runs. Apparently he used to spend more time playing cricket for the local squire's team than he did in the pub of which he was the landlord.

My schoolboy dreams turned to ashes as I realised I was more like my father whose cricketing abilities were negligible. The only story he had to tell was of being press-ganged into umpiring for the local church side who were playing away against a team in the Swansea Valley. His decisions so incensed the local supporters that after the match they chased him over the fields. In his anxiety to escape the howling mob he jumped feet first into a dung heap. His journey back to Swansea on the train was spent with his legs protruding from the open window, by order of the team.

I was practising a forward defensive stroke in the passage when Mrs Richards opened the front door, shopping bag in hand. She stood speechless, in amazement.

'It's all right, Mrs Richards,' I explained, 'I've not gone off my head. In a moment of weakness I've arranged to take the Preece boys down to the Welfare ground this afternoon to play cricket.'

'Well, I must say,' she answered, 'you really are a good Samaritan. On your day off, too.'

'I've done it to protect Mr Richards' greenhouse more than anything,' I replied. 'Lenny decided to throw his father's cricket ball over the wall and it's broken two panes of glass.'

Her face was a picture of mixed emotions – grief at the desecration of the shrine and sympathy for Mrs Preece having to cope with three young scamps singlehanded.

'It's not Lennie's fault,' she said. 'He's only little. Those other two shouldn't have let him play with it. Anyway, I'll get Roberts the Ironmonger to put the panes back.'

'Mrs Preece says she'll pay for the damage,' I told her.

'No! There's no need for that,' replied my landlady. 'She's got more than a plateful, as it is.'

'Would you like me to go and ask Mr Roberts to come down while you're getting dinner ready?' I asked.

'Thank you very much, Mr Secombe,' she said. 'There's no time like at present, as they say.'

Mr Roberts was an elderly gentleman with flowing white hair, like a Welsh Bard and with a pair of horn-rimmed spectacles, permanently fixed halfway down his nose. He wore a pair of immaculately clean brown overalls, with pockets bulging with an assortment of metal tape-measures and slide rules.

'I come on an errand of mercy for Mrs Richards, my landlady,' I announced. 'There are two broken panes of glass in the late Mr Richards' greenhouse.'

'What size are they, Reverend?' he enquired.

'No idea,' I said. 'I'm afraid I'm not good at measuring and that sort of thing. Certainly not at putting panes of glass back.'

'God gives to each one of us different talents,' he pontificated. Evidently he was chapel. 'With you it's brains, with me, it's my hands. Mind you, they are not what they were. I'll have to ask my assistant to come back with you to measure up. Excuse me.' He went to the back of the shop and shouted. 'Willie!! He's outside, stacking some timber,' he explained.

Willie appeared in a pair of brown overalls, three sizes too large for him. He looked to be about sixteen and about five foot tall.

'Will you go with the Reverend to measure two panes of glass?' asked the ironmonger.

His red-headed assistant seemed only too pleased to get out of his timber-stacking. A big grin split his little pimpled face.

'Certainly, Mr Roberts.' His voice was not yet completely broken, soprano varying with bass.

He talked incessantly all the way to my 'digs'. Apparently he had just left Pontywen Grammar School and was waiting for the results of his exams. He had great plans for the future – a career as a fighter pilot, followed by a middle age of commercial aircraft management, when he left the RAF.

'Now that the War's over, life's going to be great,' he forecast.

'I hope so,' I said. 'By the way, the man next door is in the Air Force. He's an air gunner.'

'Who's that?' he asked.

'Mr Preece,' I said.

'Oh! Danny Preece. He's great. Good cricketer,' commented Willie.

'So I gather,' I replied. 'It was his cricket ball which broke the panes of glass. His little boy threw it over the wall.'

'Starting early,' said Willie, as he measured the glass with the assurance of an expert.

'I expect Mr Roberts will ask me to put the glass in for you,' he told Mrs Richards.

'Aren't you a bit young?' asked Mrs Richards. 'Can't Mr Roberts come and do it?'

'He's a bit old,' replied the cheeky youngster. 'He doesn't do repair work these days.'

'In that case, it's Dobson's choice,' said my landlady.

Prompt on half past two, I knocked on the Preeces' front door, bat in hand and wearing an open-necked shirt, instead of my dog-collar.

Bedlam broke out in the passage. Danny, Lew and Lennie were all talking excitedly.

'Shut up!!' shouted their mother.

There was a moment's silence before she opened the door. The next minute the three boys hurtled over the steps, as if shot from a cannon. Danny was carrying four wickets, children's size. Lennie brought up the rear, chanting 'I want to be first in.'

'Now you behave yourselves, you three,' warned their mother. 'It's very good of you to take them down the Welfare like this,' she said.

'No bother, Mrs Preece,' I replied nonchalantly, with my fingers crossed over the ball in my pocket.

I thought Willie was talkative but he was nothing compared with the three lads who competed with each other for my attention every step of the way. Lennie may have been the smallest but he was possessed of the loudest voice by several decibels.

The Welfare ground was comparatively deserted for a school holiday. A couple of old men were sitting on a seat in earnest conversation, while four mongrels were under the delusion that they were on a greyhound track.

'Where shall we put up the wickets?' I asked.

'Over by there,' commanded Danny. 'There is more grass by there.'

We encountered some difficulty putting in the wickets. The ground was hard and the wickets were blunt-ended. Eventually I hammered them into position with my bat.

'I'm first in,' shouted Lennie.

'I've got first bowl,' declared Danny.

'I'm stumper,' announced Lew, taking up position behind the wickets.

'That leaves me to be nine fielders rolled into one,' I said, 'so don't hit the ball too far.'

My bat was a few inches taller than Lennie. The only way he could wield the willow was by laying it flat on the ground and then turning it sideways to face his brother's bowling.

'Not hard now, Danny,' instructed Lennie. Danny had left his single bowler's wicket and was pacing out his run.

'You'd better leave that fast bowling till I come in,' I suggested. 'Just bowl him a ball gently underarm.'

The eldest brother came back to the wicket and rolled the ball along the ground. Lennie attempted to move the bat but it went backwards instead of forwards and all three wickets were laid flat.

'Out!!' shouted Danny and Lew.

'Trial ball,' I said. 'Give him one more chance.'

Once again the stumps had to be battered in. The game was exhausting me already.

The next ball trickled over Lennie's bat and mercifully rested against the wickets without knocking them over.

'Out this time!' The two boys shouted.

'That was too hard,' objected Lennie.

'No, it wasn't,' I said. 'Your turn will come again in a minute.'

He walked away in a sulk and sat down on the grass.

'You're next, Mr Secombe,' directed Danny.

'Don't you want to bat?' I asked.

'No, I'm a bowler like my father,' he said proudly.

I picked up the bat and took guard, enjoying the pleasure of pretending to be a stylish batsman. Meanwhile Danny had taken some dozen paces from the bowling wicket. He came running up like a steam engine. Over came his arm. The ball never touched the ground but made violent contact with the most vulnerable part of my anatomy.

For a few seconds I must have passed out. When I came around the two elderly gentlemen were advancing towards me. I could see them through coloured lights. My groin was in acute agony.

'Sit up and put your head between your legs,' suggested one of them.

'Nasty that is,' said the other. 'I had that once when we played Ystrad. Always used a box after that.'

'Mr Secombe,' yelled Danny, 'that dog has gone off with my dad's ball.'

I sat up, put my head between my legs, and said a prayer of thanks that the ball had disappeared for the time being. It had caused a lot of trouble.

The two gentlemen made their way back to their seat. After sitting for a while, the pain eased sufficiently for me to stand up. I was aware of Lennie looking at me, greatly concerned for my welfare.

'Are you better, Mr Secombe?' he asked.

'Oh, I'm fine now,' I said. 'Where are Danny and Lew?'

'They've gone to get the ball from that dog,' he replied. 'Can I have another go with the bat?'

'I don't feel very well,' I told him. 'Let's sit on the seat until they come back.'

We walked slowly to another seat some distance from the two old men. Lennie's company was preferable.

'Can I hold the bat?' he asked.

'Of course,' I replied.

'It's a big bat this one,' the little boy said, 'like my dad's.' He stroked it. 'My dad will be coming back from India soon. He goes up in aeroplanes, with a machine gun.' He dropped the bat and did an imitation of firing a machine gun. As he moved into his third 'brrr', I could see Will Book and Pencil striding across the ground.

The Constable reached our seat in no time.

'Trouble, Reverend,' he murmured looking at the boy.

'Lennie,' I said. 'You look after my bat while I go and have a talk with the policeman.'

We walked down the path a little way.

'It's his father, I'm afraid,' said the Constable. I've just had to bring the news to his mother that her husband has been killed in a flying accident in India.' She told me the boys were down here with you.'

I felt the same kind of shock as when a family, further up the street in which I lived, was wiped out by a bomb in an

86

air raid on Swansea. My stomach turned over. I was unable to speak.

'She wants the boys back with her,' went on Will. 'I told her that I'd get you to bring them back. Perhaps you can help a bit in the situation.'

'Keep a grip on yourself,' I told myself. 'If you can't do that first, you can't do anything.'

I swallowed hard.

'How er – is she taking it?' I asked.

'Too shocked to think at the moment,' replied Will. 'But I expect she'll cope because of the boys. Women are much tougher than men.'

'What on earth is she going to say to the children?' I said, more to myself, than to the policeman.

'Well, that's where you can help,' suggested Will. 'I'd better be off before the two older boys come and start asking questions about why I'm here.'

'That's Will Book and Pencil, isn't it?' said Lennie. 'He puts people in jail when they're naughty, Mam says.'

Evidently he had been threatened by his mother with the law to try and make him behave.

At that moment Danny and Lew came bounding across the Welfare Ground. Danny was holding his father's cricket ball in triumph, above his head.

'We caught him down by the gate,' he announced between gasps.

'I held him,' added Lew, 'and Danny got the ball out of his mouth.'

'I'm afraid, boys,' I said, 'we've got to go back. I'm not feeling very well.'

'Sorry about hitting you, Mr Secombe,' apologised Danny. 'I tried to bowl a yorker.'

'You certainly yorked me,' I replied.

'Can I carry the wickets?' asked Lennie.

'All right,' said Danny, 'and I'll carry the ball.'

'In that case, Lew,' I said. 'You can carry the bat.'

The four of us made our way back up the hill to the house. Conversation was non-stop between the three boys. It was just as well since I found the journey increasingly foreboding.

I knocked on the door, my heart pounding. To my surprise, it was opened by Mrs Richards.

'Come on in boys,' she said. 'Your mother's resting in the front room. I've got some cakes for you in the kitchen. Put all those cricket things away first.'

'You can keep the bat for the time being,' I told them.

'Out the back you go,' commanded my landlady.

When they had disappeared, she said, 'Terrible news, wasn't it? I saw Will Book and Pencil knock on the door. I thought it was something dramatic. So I came round after he'd gone. I've made her a cup of tea. I think she'll be glad to see you.'

Mrs Richards tapped on the front-room door and ushered me in. Her neighbour sat on a chair, looking out through the window with the same vacant stare I had seen on the faces of the women in the workhouse, eyes like windows in an empty house.

'Mrs Preece, I'm very sorry about the news,' I ventured. 'You have my deepest sympathy.'

She turned her face towards me. It was ashen.

'Thank you, Mr Secombe,' she replied. 'I can't take it in yet. It's just like a bad dream. I was looking forward to him coming home so much.'

'What about the boys?' I asked. 'I suppose it's early to think about how you are going to tell them.'

'I can't think at the moment,' she said. 'Maybe I'll send them down to my mother in Cardiff out of the way, pretending it's a holiday for them. She's a widow living alone in a four-bedroomed house. She'll be glad of the company.'

That is what happened. It was a long holiday for the boys. They never came back. Mrs Preece joined them, moving to Cardiff to escape from memories which were inescapable.

Later that evening Willie arrived at my digs with the panes of glass and a bag of Mr Roberts' tools. After he had finished his work and presented Mr Roberts' bill to Mrs Richards, he said, 'Dreadful news about Danny Preece, isn't it?'

'Do you still want to be a pilot?' I asked.

'If I'd been in charge of that plane, it wouldn't have crashed,' he replied.

'You remember, young man,' said my landlady, 'pride goes in front of a fall.'

'Very apt, Mrs Richards,' I said.

8

'Have you heard about Protheroe the Butcher?' enquired Mrs Richards at breakfast.

'What about him?' I said.

'You know those old Russian flags with the hammer and the scythe on it? Well, he put one of them in the pig's head that he's got in his window. He's true Blue and he can't stand those Communionists. Will Book and Pencil had to go up and ask him to take it out because of complaints.'

There were plenty of those old Russian flags about in Pontywen Square, as well as Union Jacks and tired-looking bunting. It was VJ Day and I had now settled quietly into the parish after that first eventful week. By extreme forbearance on my part, I had achieved a modicum of rapport with the Vicar. Indeed on one occasion he asked my help in solving the *Daily Telegraph* crossword. My contact with the 'Vicaress' had been minimal.

Pontywen's version of VJ celebrations was due to take place that evening. The local bigwigs led by Councillor David Waters, alias 'Dai Spout', decided on a display of fireworks. Instead of arranging the spectacle in the rugby ground, the special committee thought it more appropriate to have it in the town centre, 'the heart of the Community', as Dai Spout put it.

Pontywen boasted a free-standing town clock, a gift from a coal baron. 'Conscience money paid for that,' said Idris the Milk as we passed it on my first Sunday in the parish. The clock stood in the middle of a square, surrounded by shops.

The newly elected Labour MP had promised to attend the display before going down the Valley to visit other functions.

To enable the VIP to keep to his timetable, the fireworks were timed to begin at seven p.m. in broad daylight. This was a matter of little consequence to 'Dai Spout', as long as the MP could be present.

Mrs Richards had refused my offer to escort her to the big event.

'I'm too old to go and see fireworks,' she said. 'In any case, I should have thought there were enough bangs and descendaries in the war.'

'It's bound to be eventful,' I said to Idris. 'Bertie Owen is in charge of the fireworks. Well, so he said, last Sunday.'

'God 'elp us, in that case,' commented the milkman.

We took up our position outside Moelwyn the Fruiterer's.

'If we stand by 'ere on the doorstep,' said Idris, 'we won't be pushed and shoved.'

It was sound advice. Before long the square was crowded with people spilling over from the pavement into the road. Several were full of alcoholic good cheer.

Elsie, the cherub, was perched on her father's shoulder, Percy managed to stand on the sill of the fruiterer's shop, supporting himself by using me as a prop. Gwen was standing on tiptoe, her eyes glued on the town clock.

Trestle tables were set up at the base of the clock, on which reposed the fireworks. Jones the Wireless shop had his loudspeaker van parked alongside – fresh from its use in last month's election campaign. Dai Spout and his wife, now fully recovered from her operation, occupied centre stage among the committee as they waited for the MP to arrive.

Suddenly, there was a crackle over the loudspeaker. A voice said, 'Testing – one, two, three. Mary had a little watch, she swallowed it one day. Now she's taking Beecham's pills to pass the time away. Is that OK, Norman?'

'That's Bertie, the stupid . . .' Idris swallowed the next word. 'He's had a few. 'E's only got to smell the barmaid's apron and 'e's gone. Dai Spout will 'ave 'is guts for garters.'

Any further conversation was forestalled by the cheers which greeted the arrival of the MP Gwynfor Williams. It was his first public appearance in Pontywen since the election and he made the most of it. He acknowledged the cheers by holding his arms aloft, as if he had just won the war single-handed.

Councillor David Waters proceeded to the microphone. 'I'm sure you will want me to say a few words,' he began.

Groans were heard from all quarters.

'To congratulate our newly elected Member of Parliament on his great victory. Twenty-two thousand majority. A new world is beginning. From now on the working man will have his due, his fair share, his right to a decent wage . . .'

As Dai Spout moved into top gear, it looked as if he would not surrender the microphone for the rest of the evening. Gwynfor Williams, MP, kept consulting his watch, scratching his head and occasionally looking up at the heavens as if asking for a thunderbolt to cut off the councillor in his prime.

Gradually the crowd began to render that well-known hymn 'Why are we waiting?' Elsie, in her boredom, on her father's shoulder, began an incessant chant of 'When's the fireworks, Dad?'

To the relief of everybody and especially the MP, Dai, Spout wound up his introduction by saying, 'And now I give you the man you are waiting to hear.'

'Not another lot,' I said to Idris.

''E don't speak very much,' he replied. 'They say that the only thing 'e's said in the whole of the last two Parliaments is, 'Will you close the window because it's draughty?''

Idris was right. In three sentences, the Member of Parliament thanked the people for electing him, the boys for winning the War and the committee for arranging the fireworks. Then he went off in his car to repeat the same message several times down the Valley.

Dai Spout was back at the microphone. 'I'm sure you don't want to hear me any more,' he said.

'No!' shouted a thousand voices.

'Well, I have great pleasure in declaring these fireworks open.'

Bertie Owen stepped forward and seized the microphone.

'I hope you all enjoy the splendid show we've got for you,' he bellowed, causing the equipment to whistle. 'We begin with some rockets. Watch for the coloured stars and wait for the bangs.'

'Wait for it,' said Idris.

Bertie disappeared behind some form of a home-made ramp on which were visible the heads of half a dozen rockets.

'Light the blue touchpaper and retire,' I said to Idris. 'It looks as if Bertie has retired before he's lit it.' As I finished speaking, a rocket crawled lazily into the air and collapsed into the fireworks on the trestle table.

The next second all hell broke loose. Rockets were shooting sideways instead of upwards. Explosions seemed to be happening throughout Pontywen. Amid screams and shouts, everybody was lying on the ground in self protection. Elsie was lying underneath me, her Union Jack stuck in the back of my clerical collar. Percy was buried at the base of a scrum on the pavement, while Idris was acting as a shield for Gwen.

There was an almighty crack as Protheroe's plate-glass window felt the impact of a rocket head. A kaleidoscope of coloured smoke filled the square as the last few bangs went off sporadically. Then came an eerie silence as everyone waited for the next explosion which never arrived.

One by one, the crowd of spectators got to their feet. Soon the air was filled with the noise of those who were relieved to find they were still intact. Bertie Owen had achieved something Hitler could not do. He had put the fear of God into the populace of Pontywen who had never heard a bomb or seen an incendiary during the whole of the War.

Bedraggled Committee men dusted down their best suits and the ladies their summer frocks. Mrs Dai Spout's dyed hair was in a mess. The expression on her face was murderous but not quite as murderous as that on her husband's face.

'I think Dai Spout is going to hang Bertie from the top of the town clock,' said Idris.

'He'll have plenty of helpers,' I said.

'My one and only pair of nylons is ruined, thanks to Bertie,' complained Gwen.

'When is the fireworks going to begin?' asked Elsie waving a Union Jack with half a stick.

The Councillor strode to the loudspeaker van. There was no sign of Bertie who must have made a quick exit to escape being lynched.

'I must apologise for the – er – unfortunate accident. These

things do happen sometimes. Thank you all for coming, anyway.'

That was the shortest and most memorable speech Dai Spout ever made in his life.

For a few weeks Bertie Owen kept a low profile – quite a feat for him. However, by the first Sunday in September, he was back to his normal self. I had the usual ticktack signs from the back of the church and the sidesmen were subjected to his military discipline.

The following evening, Bertie appeared on my doorstep. His car was parked outside, minus glass on one headlamp and with a slightly buckled wing.

'Can I see you urgently, Mr Secombe?' he said anxiously. 'I don't want to worry the Vicar, he's too old for this sort of thing, but I am sure you can help. You're a good talker.'

When he sat down in my armchair, I asked him, 'What sort of thing is the Vicar too old for and how can I help?'

'It's like this,' he began. 'Well, yesterday morning after Church, we counted up the money. Very good, by the way, ten pounds three and seven pence halfpenny, sixty-two communicants and quite a few strangers. Numbers are still keeping up since you have been here, thank God.'

He beamed at me, forgetting his anxiety for a moment.

Then his eyes clouded.

'Well, as I was saying,' he went on. 'You know I take Mrs Bradshaw home, the one with the bad legs. Walks slowly like a penguin, you know her.' He demonstrated her walk with his hands. 'Well, I got her into the front seat with a bit of a struggle. After all, she must weigh about twenty stone. She can't get in the back seat, can't get through the door. Well, I got her in and then I put the collection money on the shelf by the dashboard, over where she was sitting. Then we started off for Melrose Avenue . . . That's where she lives – we came to the roundabout by The Lamb and Flag.' He paused, either for breath or dramatic effect.

'Well, as we were going round the roundabout, the money fell out of the shelf. I carried on driving with my right hand and tried to pick up the money from Mrs Bradshaw's lap with my left hand. The next I knew was that we were up on the island and I had knocked the ball-yard over.'

The picture of Bertie and Mrs Bradshaw stranded on a desert island in Pontywen with Bertie's hand in her lap, was too much for me. I had a fit of coughing which necessitated the use of my handkerchief. When it stopped, Bertie carried on.

'Well, I took her home when I got the car down off the island. She was all right, a bit shocked like. So she gave me some whisky which she keeps for medical purposes and had some herself. Then I drove down to Will Book and Pencil, the policeman at the police box, to report the accident. That's why I've come to see you.' He stared at me anxiously.

'You are telling me, that you went to Will the policeman, smelling of whisky, to report your accident,' I said. 'That was a bit risky, wasn't it?'

'Well, I explained to him that it was for medical purposes,' he replied, 'and I told him that if I hadn't tried to pick up the money from Mrs Bradshaw's lap while I was driving, there wouldn't have been any accident with the ball-yard because I was driving slowly at the time. But he says he's got to report me for careless driving and I was wondering if you could do anything about it.'

'I'll do what I can to help, Bertie,' I said. 'I'm afraid you have landed yourself in trouble by admitting to the policeman that you were driving carelessly and by smelling of whisky while you were telling him.'

'I wasn't driving carelessly,' Bertie answered. 'I was driving quite slowly.'

'However slowly you were driving,' I told him, 'you cannot drive and pick up money from somebody else's lap at the same time. You should have stopped the car first.'

'I'll tell you what,' he said, 'I won't do it again.'

'That's not the point,' I replied. 'We must do what we can now to get you out of this trouble. I'll see Will tomorrow.'

'Thank you very much.' The furrows left his brow and it was obvious that he thought he had been given freedom from prosecution already.

'Don't take it for granted that I can do anything,' I warned him.

'No, Mr Secombe,' he said with a vacuous smile.

It was a very unconvincing 'no'.

Next morning, I called in at the police box to see Will Book and Pencil who was having an argument with Moelwyn the Fruiterer about a lorry which had been parked outside his shop for too long, according to Will. It was obvious that the policeman was in a bad mood. The book and pencil were much in evidence. I thought of calling again but the 'law' had seen me waiting. It was too late to escape.

'Hallo, Mr Secombe! What can I do for you?' he asked in a brusque tone. Then he added. 'Moelwyn, I'll see you later.' Moelwyn's moustache twitched with apprehension.

Will sat on the stool by the ledge of the box and still towered over me. It was most intimidating.

'It's about Bertie Owen,' I said tentatively.

'Oh, that dull bugger, if you'll pardon the expression, Mr Secombe,' replied the policeman. 'I've made out a report but I don't think they'll prosecute. He'll probably have a letter from the Chief warning him that if there is a next time, there'll be a prosecution.'

I called at Bertie's house that night to tell him that most

likely there would be no prosecution. Mrs Owen opened the door. She was a large woman, even more intimidating than Will Book and Pencil.

'Fortunately,' I said, 'it looks as if there will be no prosecution.'

'Thank God for that,' she replied. 'He'd be doing his nut if he had to go to Court. He worried enough about the fireworks.'

A few minutes later, Bertie arrived home to be greeted by the smell of liver and onions and the news of his reprieve.

His gratitude knew no bounds.

'Thank you very much, Mr Secombe,' he said, beaming like the Mumbles lighthouse. He shook my hand several times.

'I tell you what,' he continued, 'I know you're having driving lessons in the Vicar's car. Would you like me to give you some in mine?'

I could feel the hairs on the back of my neck standing up.

'That's very kind, Bertie,' I said. 'But if you don't mind, I have to refuse the offer. Mervyn from the garage is teaching me, as you know, and I don't think he would be very pleased if somebody else was going to give me lessons as well.'

'How about a bike?' he asked. 'You haven't got transport. A bike would be helpful, wouldn't it?'

'It would indeed,' I replied, 'but I have never ridden one.'

'Oh, it's as easy as falling off a horse, if you know what I mean,' said Bertie enthusiastically. 'The point is, I've got a bike I don't use now I've got the car. You can borrow that permanently, like.'

The next evening I was practising riding the bicycle up and down Mount Pleasant View. By the time I had fallen off twice and collided with a lamppost, I had attracted a fair-sized audience in the open doorways.

'Why don't you take the bike down the Rec?' Suggested Llew Williams from number ten. He came up to me as I was clinging to the lamppost. 'It won't be so dangerous for you when you do fall off – and there's no lampposts down there.' He looked around at the grinning faces in the street. 'Nor spectators if it comes to that,' he said in confidential tones.

The recreation ground was a piece of wasteland some

streets away, down in the valley. It was used by small boys during the day and by courting couples after dark.

I trundled Bertie's bike down the road to find the 'Rec' deserted. At the price of several bruises and a grazed shin, I learnt the art of riding a bicycle in an hour's cavorting round the perimeter of the ground.

As darkness and the first courting couple approached, I ventured to ride through three streets without falling off.

At the end of Inkerman street, I encountered Full-Back Jones.

'You're riding that bike like an old woman,' he said, grinning like a toothless old hag himself.

'I've never ridden a bike before,' I replied in high dudgeon.

'I can see that,' he said. 'It's practice you want – out on the country roads.'

I was to get that sooner than I thought.

'I gather you have acquired a bicycle from Bertie Owen,' said the Vicar. He paused and growled, ' – for favours received. I wish you would let me know when you make official representations to the police on somebody else's behalf.'

My hackles rose and I found such great difficulty in controlling them that it was painful.

'Quite frankly, Vicar, I did not think you would have been concerned to know about it. As for the favour, I had no ulterior motive in helping Bertie. I wasn't even aware that he had a bicycle.'

'Don't get on your high horse, Secombe.' He was taken aback by my reaction. 'This is my parish and I want to know what is happening in it. So from now on, please let me know when something like this happens.'

'I shall take great care to see that you are kept informed from now on.'

The edge in my voice provoked him.

'Don't be sarcastic, young man,' he rasped. 'In any case, if it takes you as long to learn how to ride a bicycle as it does to drive a car, it will be some time before it's of use.'

'As a matter of fact, Vicar,' I said, 'I have learnt how to ride it already.'

He raised his eyebrows.

'In that case, you can save me a journey. The Rural Dean wants to borrow some Confirmation veils for his female Candidates. It's an opportunity for you to meet him. I'll get my wife to put the veils in a shopping bag which you can sling over the handlebars.'

When Mrs Llewellyn appeared some minutes later, she had a leather shopping bag with her.

'Tell Mrs Thomas that I have washed and ironed the veils,' she said in vinegary tones. 'All I hope is that you get them there safely – after your car experiences.'

With this vote of confidence ringing in my ears, I left the Vicarage for the more congenial pastures of Mount Pleasant View.

'I have to go to Pentwyn this afternoon, Mrs Richards, to the Rural Dean. I'm going on the bike,' I said, not without a certain amount of self importance.'

'You be careful, Mr Secombe,' she warned. 'It's a nasty old road, full of bends, once you get off the main road. The Vicarage is at the bottom of a steep hill. I only hope Bertie Owen's machine has got its brakes going.'

Apparently the Reverend Daniel Thomas, BA, RD, was seldom seen outside his parish. The only time his Clergy saw him was at the clergy meeting which closed down for the summer months. It was to resume next week.

My cycle journey, on the main road, was uneventful. There was little traffic and I kept as close to the kerb as I possibly could. Eventually, I came to a signpost indicating that Pentwyn was one mile away, off the main road.

Mrs Richards was right. The road was not only full of bends but climbed steeply. I dismounted and pushed the bicycle up the incline. On reaching the top, I could see the tower of the old mediaeval church at the foot of the hill.

I re-mounted the machine and made my way down, applying the brakes for dear life. As I came round the last bend I could see the entrance to the Vicarage drive about fifty yards away. In my relief at seeing my destination so close, I relaxed my iron grip on the brakes. As the bicycle gathered speed, a sheepdog appeared from nowhere with an urgent desire to attack me.

I was faced with an equally urgent decision. Either I stopped and was attacked or I sailed into the Vicarage drive and escaped the dog. I chose the latter course.

Seconds later I was lying on the drive, looking into a grey, wrinkled face which was dominated by a large, squashed proboscis.

'Mr – er – Seaton?' enquired the Rural Dean. 'Your Vicar said you were coming.'

Evidently he was accustomed to greeting prone cyclists. As an afterthought, he said, 'Are you all right? It's that stone just inside the entrance. You'd be surprised how often I forget it's there and bump into it with the car.'

As he was helping me to my feet, I was about to ask him why he had not moved the stone but swallowed the question out of deference to his position.

Bertie's bicycle seemed to be intact but the leather shopping bag had been badly scratched by the gravel on the drive. A vision of Mrs Llewellyn's face arose like that of a grisly spectre.

It was driven away by the appearance of a rosy-cheeked, silver-haired and comfortably upholstered lady. 'This is my wife,' said the Rural Dean. She seized my hand with a grip of iron.

'Welcome to Pentwyn,' she said warmly. 'You must come and have a cup of tea to settle your nerves. Thank you for bringing the veils.'

'Mrs Llewellyn says that they are washed and ironed,' I said. 'I think they are OK; they didn't fall out of the bag.'

'Don't worry about that, my dear,' she replied. 'I'm sure they are perfect, if Mrs Llewellyn has done them.' There were slight overtones of sarcasm in that remark.

I pushed the bicycle up the drive and parked it beside the door of the big Victorian Vicarage. I looked out over a vast, immaculately kept lawn. At the back of the house was a small wood, while lining the drive and the lawn were Lombardy poplar trees. Elegance worthy of a rural dean, I thought.

'What lovely grounds you have,' I said.

'Lovely, as long as you don't have to cut the lawn,' said the Rural Dean. 'You wait. You'll find out one of these days. Won't he, Arianwen?'

Arianwen agreed.

'Well, come on in, Mr Seabourne,' he said.

The inside of the house was as elegant as the grounds. To a Curate whose 'digs' were in Mount Pleasant View, it represented a standard of living as remote as life on Mars.

Arianwen brought us tea in the expensively furnished drawing room.

'Well, Mr Seagrove,' said the Rural Dean, through his nose, 'how are you settling down in Pontywen?'

'I think I shall be quite happy there,' I replied. 'There's plenty to do and I hate being idle.'

'Canon Llewellyn will keep you busy, no doubt. He's a great one for training curates. I've never had curates. They say there's only one thing worse than not having a curate and that's having a curate.' He paused. Realising that he was talking to one of the despised species, he added, 'Mind, I'm sure that doesn't apply to you, Mr Seebohm.'

I thought the time had come to give the dignitary my correct name.

'Excuse me,' I said, 'but my name is Secombe.'

I spelt it out for him.

'I beg your pardon, young man,' he answered, carefully avoiding the danger of pronouncing my name. 'By the way, we have our Chapter meeting in the back-room of the Bull Inn in Tremadoc next Monday.'

'That sounds very convivial,' I said heartily.

'No! No! It's not what you think. We meet after closing time, in the afternoon. Then we have tea and cakes when we finish the meeting. I'm afraid you will be the only curate but you will find the fellows will make you very welcome.' He seemed anxious to point out what a sober lot of 'fellows' there were in his deanery.

After I had consumed three cups of tea, he asked, 'Would you like to make yourself comfortable?'

'If you don't mind,' I replied.

He led me out from the room, down a corridor and then flung open a door.

'Here's the Secombe, Mr Cloakroom,' he proclaimed.

The following Monday, at three p.m., the local bus deposited me outside the Bull in Tremadoc, as the last regulars were crawling out of the saloon bar. My Vicar had decided that he had too much to do in his parish and asked me to present his apologies.

I pushed my way into the saloon bar and bumped into the landlord as he was on his way to close the doors.

'Closing time long ago, sir,' he said. I removed the scarf

from my neck to reveal my clerical collar. 'Sorry, Reverend!' he exclaimed. 'The other reverend gentlemen are around the back. I'll take you through but next time go round to the back entrance through the yard.'

He led me through a small maze of passages until we reached a glass door from behind which there came faint murmurs of conversation. 'This is it, sir,' he said.

I opened the door and beheld the oddest assortment of clergy I had ever seen. One elderly cleric, obviously in his eighties, was stretched out, fast asleep, in an armchair. Next to him, almost lost in another armchair, was a tiny clergyman who looked even older, like a gnome who had strayed from the garden. Seated by the blazing hearth on a tall carved chair suitable for a bishop's throne, was the Rural Dean. On the other side of the hearth, on a kitchen chair, was a tall, thin, bespectacled man in his fifties, a veritable babe. He was evidently the Chapter Clerk since he had an opened exercise book on his lap and a notepad on the floor at his feet. By his side, seated on the edge of an armchair, bolt upright and resembling a startled rabbit, was another thin man, in his seventies. On his knees was a small suitcase which must have had very valuable contents, judging by the way he hugged it.

There was a vacant armchair by the rabbit. 'Take a seat, young man,' said the Rural Dean with a smile and an expansive gesture. Obviously he was in a jovial mood.

'This is the new curate of Pontywen,' he announced. 'If you don't mind,' he went on, 'I will introduce you later. We are about to have the minutes of the last meeting. Carry on, Mr Morris.'

Mr Morris stood up, with the exercise book in his hand. 'Minutes of the last meeting held at The Bull Inn, Tremadoc, on the third of October, beginning at three o seven p.m.' It took him a couple of minutes to say that sentence. I had never heard anyone drawl a sentence so slowly. The recumbent clergyman opposite me snored loudly – so loudly that he woke himself up. He half opened two bleary blue eyes, on either side of his purple nose. The eyes focused on me. Fascinated, I stared at him. A faint smile emerged on his florid countenance – only to fade as his eyelids closed again.

Meanwhile, the Chapter Clerk had managed to read a

couple of sentences. There followed a long pause as he tried to cope with turning over a page. There was an even longer pause after he had done so. Then he said, 'Sorry, Mr Rural Dean, I have turned over two pages at once.'

'Like the Vicar who turned over two pages at once!' guffawed the Rural Dean.

This was enough to awaken the sleeping Clergyman who opened wide his eyes, stared at me and gave me another faint smile. Slowly, he closed his eyes and resumed his slumbers.

The Reverend Morris, Chapter Clerk, dragged out the minutes. There was an audible sigh of relief from the four of us who were more or less awake as he staggered past the finishing post.

'All in favour,' said the Rural Dean. There was a faint murmur.

'Now then, Mr Williams-Evans,' he went on, addressing the holder of the suitcase. 'What have you got for us to see?'

'What, indeed?' I said to myself. Was the Reverend Williams-Evans doing a sideline in jewellery for Clergy wives or clerical garments for members of the Chapter?

My speculations were dispelled as the Rural Dean addressed me. 'Mr Seabourne,' he said, 'our friend here goes down to Cardiff in July, to get books that we can have a look at before choosing one for next year's study.'

Gingerly, the clerical rabbit opened his case and silently passed around a number of paperback books.

The Rural Dean picked on the slimmest of the volumes. 'This looks about the right size for us,' he said, waving it aloft.

The Reverend William-Evans raised his eyes and spoke for the first and only time that afternoon.

'That's the catalogue, Mr Rural Dean,' he replied.

'So it is. So it is,' said the Rural Dean, quite unabashed.

The books were passed hand to hand over the inert body in the one armchair. None of them was particularly enthralling and none of them was examined for more than a minute.

'Here's one!' shouted the Rural Dean triumphantly. He brandished the copy and added, 'It's only three and six. All in favour?'

Four hands shot up.

'That's it, then,' he said. 'Now then, Mr Morris, will you read the last Chapter of our book for this year?'

The garden gnome disappeared into his armchair and prepared to join his friend in slumber. For the three of us who were awake, it was a test of endurance as we listened to the Chapter Clerk drawl through the last chapter on the Athanasian Creed.

As he came to the end of the last sentence, the Reverend Daniel Thomas, BA, RD, enquired, 'Any comments?'

If any one had been imbecile enough to make one, he would have been cut off in his prime.

'Thank you,' said the Chairman in the same breath as his query. He rubbed his hands in front of the fire. 'Now then, we'll have some tea and cakes.'

That was the signal for our sleeping partner to awake. Like Rip Van Winkle, he came to life again, stretched his arms and sat upright in his chair. He looked across the room at me, as if he had never seen me before.

'Are you the Speaker?' he asked.

The Rural Dean intervened.

'No, Mr Hughes,' he said. 'This is the Reverend Seagrove, who has come to Pontywen.'

'What's happened to Llewellyn, then?' enquired Rip Van Winkle.

The Rural Dean's patience was wearing thin.

'Nothing has happened to Llewellyn. This is his new Curate,' he snapped.

'Oh!' said Mr Hughes. 'Is the tea ready?'

'I think it would be a good idea, young man,' said the Rural Dean, ignoring Mr Hughes, and placing his arm round my shoulders, 'if you started off the study of the new book by doing the first chapter. You are more up to date than the rest of the fellows.'

Since two of the 'fellows' were old enough to be my great grandfather, it was no great compliment.

'Thank you for asking me, Mr Rural Dean,' I said. 'I took my degree in history and since the book is about the early Church, I shall be very interested in it.'

'Good, good,' he said. 'If you haven't got the three and six on you now, Mr Williams-Evans will collect it from you at the next meeting. We get credit, you see. Mr Williams-Evans, will you let Mr Seagrove have the book? Mr Morris, will you collect the shillings for the tea?'

He pulled out his pocket watch from his waistcoat and gave it a long, searching look, as if he were examining a pearl of great price.

'A parting present from my last parish, Gold hunter,' he said to me. 'Twenty-seven years ago. They don't make 'em like that any more. Where's that woman with our tea and cakes?'

He opened the door and bawled into the empty corridor.

'We're ready, Mrs Matthews.'

As the reverberations of his roar were dying away, there came an almighty crash of china and metal. Some sopranos can break a glass with a top C. Evidently, the Rural Dean's voice could shatter a load of tea cups at a distance of yards and through two brick walls.

Mr Morris dropped the three shillings he had collected and Mr Williams-Evans' case dropped from his bony knees, scattering the books from Cardiff over the floor.

'Sounds like an accident,' said the garden gnome. It was his first utterance that afternoon.

'Stop collecting, Mr Morris,' ordered the Rural Dean. 'Perhaps that's the end of our tea. I'll go and enquire.'

He was back in no time.

'I'm afraid that's it,' he announced. 'The cups are broken and the cakes likewise. Better luck next time. I declare this meeting closed.'

It took a minute to arouse Mr Hughes who had gone back to sleep. A few minutes later we had left The Bull Inn, leaving Mrs Matthews to pick up the pieces and count the cost of entertaining the clergy.

10

'There's a letter for you,' said Mrs Richards. Apart from the weekly epistle from my parents and the occasional circular from the clerical outfitters, a letter was a rare event.

This one was in a grubby envelope, addressed to 'Reverend F. T. Secombe MA.' To someone who was merely a BA, it indicated that the writer was either intent on flattery or careless in reading the clerical directory.

Inside was an even grubbier sheet of notepaper; a bilious yellow from a pad to be seen on Woolworth counters. It was headed 'Abercoed Vicarage, Abercoed, Telephone c/o Abercoed Station'. There was no date. The writing appeared to have been the work of an intoxicated spider.

'Dear young friend,' it went on, 'I understand from one of my parishioners who heard you preach, that you can deliver a powerful sermon. You are just the one I want for my gift day – something that will make those farmers dig into their pockets. The Gift Day is Sunday week, 11th August, 6.30 p.m. You will be welcome to have a bite in the Vicarage afterwards. Yours sincerely, James Podmore, Vicar.'

The name Podmore rang a bell. I remembered an apocryphal story that one of my fellow students told me about him. His parish was in a remote rural area of the county. Its only link with civilisation was the railway station.

It seems that one morning The Reverend James Podmore arose from his bed and surveyed his domain from his bedroom window. To his annoyance he saw a donkey lying on the Vicarage lawn. He went down in his pyjamas to drive the beast away. As he emerged shouting wildly from his front door the donkey gave no sign of being aroused from its slumbers and, on closer inspection, it became evident that the beast was dead.

An irate Reverend James Podmore stalked down the road in his pyjamas to Abercoed Station and telephoned the County Borough Surveyor who, by a strange coincidence, was also named Podmore. To the further annoyance of the Reverend Podmore he was told that his namesake was out on his rounds.

So the Reverend Podmore wrote to Mr Podmore reporting that there was a dead donkey on the Vicarage lawn and asking him to make arrangements immediately to dispose of the animal. A few days later a letter arrived for the Reverend James Podmore. The County Surveyor stated that he always understood that it was the duty of the clergy to bury the dead. Forthwith, the Vicar wrote back, pointing out that it was also the duty of the clergy to inform the relatives.

An encounter with the Reverend James Podmore would be an experience to treasure. There was one snag, a big snag. The letter was addressed to me and not to the Vicar, my employer – a grave breach of clerical etiquette. I could imagine Canon Llewellyn's face when I handed him the invitation. Undoubtedly he will refuse his permission, I told myself, but at least he will see that somebody thought that I could preach a powerful sermon.

My Vicar's reaction was quite unexpected. He looked at the envelope, grunted and said, 'Podmore's Gift Day has come round once again.' The yellow notepaper was extracted with a repugnance which indicated that a pair of tongs would have been preferable to fingers.

He glanced at its contents. 'Same old ploy – powerful sermon heard by one of his congregation. Same old mistake in the date. It's the twelfth on Sunday, not the eleventh. Another experience for you, Secombe. Price had to endure it. So must you.' He looked up and gave me one of his penetrating stares.

'Write and tell him that your Vicar has given his permission grudgingly. Tell him, too, that if ever the occasion arises that he wants a further powerful sermon from you, he must write to me and not to you.'

Suddenly the prospect of meeting the Reverend James

Podmore had lost its attraction. I was not a powerful preacher any more than I was an MA.

On Sunday 12th, August I cycled to Abercoed about seven miles away from my digs, with my clerical gear contained in my battered ex-college suitcase, dangling precariously over the handlebars of my borrowed bicycle. By the time I reached the church I was liberally bedewed with perspiration. It was a very warm day.

I decided to look round the church before going to the Vicarage. As I opened the door, my nostrils were assaulted by a powerful smell, manufactured by a combination of dust, ancient stonework and the oil in the hanging lamps. The building was devoid of any beauty, cluttered with pews made of cheap wood, crying out to be varnished. To my astonishment, on the altar, with its tatty green frontal, there reposed Remembrance Day poppies in dirty brass vases. Evidently they had been there for at least seven months. It might have been seven years – and I had to conjure money out of the tight-fisted parishioners who could not spare enough even for a bunch of flowers!

A rickety unpainted gate guarded the Vicarage drive. I undid the piece of cord which fastened it to the post and made my way up the dusty path between a wilderness of bushes and overgrown grass on either side of it. I expected to be attacked by a jungle tiger at any minute.

The front door had one of those antiquated bell pulls at the side. I pulled on it and produced a deafening silence. After a couple of attempts to make it work, I gave up and banged on the door. Footsteps echoed as if in a mediaeval hall. The door creaked open and revealed the Reverend James Podmore, in his shirt sleeves, with his clerical collar half done up and hanging like a slipped question mark on his chest.

'You're early, boy,' he said. 'Come on in.' I preferred the smell of the church to the smell of that house. Onions, stale tobacco smoke, oil and dust provided the aroma. He took me into a room which served as a lounge cum study.

'Sit down and make yourself comfortable,' boomed the Vicar. 'You haven't got a cigarette on you by any chance? I've run out of mine. A Woodbine would do.'

'I'm afraid I don't smoke,' I said.

I sat down in an armchair which had seen better days. One of the springs impressed itself on my posterior.

'Relax now, boy,' he said, 'while I get the meal ready for after church. One of the penalties of being a widower. Get married, lad, as soon as you can.'

'If I sit here much longer,' I thought to myself, 'I shall be permanently injured and incapable of marriage.'

'Do you mind if I have a look round the church?' I asked, in desperation.

'You carry on, boy,' he replied.

I did. The spring propelled me from the seat like a bullet from a gun. I was through the door and into the fresh air in no time, greatly relieved. There was only one problem now: how to escape as quickly as possible after the service.

At six twenty-five p.m., I and a young schoolgirl seated at the harmonium were the only two people in church. She was attempting to play the Londonderry Air. Ten minutes later, the Vicar arrived wearing what appeared to be an engine driver's regulation denim jacket.

'They're never on time here, boy,' he said. 'What with milking and what have you. You've met Linda, I suppose.' He put his arm around the organist. 'Only fourteen she is and helping us out every Sunday these days.'

By six fifty p.m., the service got under way. There were no more than a dozen, a few hard-bitten farmers and farm labourers plus wives, in the congregation. Two of the ladies had a competition to see who could sing the loudest and the fastest, while the fourteen-year-old girl at the harmonium was coming in a poor third.

No sooner had the Vicar begun to read the first lesson than the door at the back opened and a red-faced farmer stood on the threshold frozen with embarrassment, as twelve heads turned towards him. The Reverend James Podmore stopped his reading and looked up.

'Come on in, Mr Evans,' shouted the parson. 'Half a loaf is better than none. And God spoke to Abraham and said . . .'

Before announcing the hymn before the Sermon, the Vicar harangued his congregation about their meanness.

'The Churchwardens have been suffering from copper

poisoning through counting the collections every Sunday,' he said. 'Perhaps you will remedy that today.'

'And now,' he went on, 'I should like to pass a hearty vote of thanks to our young friend who has made such a long journey here this evening. I hope you will listen to what he has to say and let the moths out of your purses.'

After such an introduction, I felt anything I had to say was superfluous. The congregation were more interested in passing sweets among themselves than in any Sermon. At least two were looking at their watches after I had been going for only five minutes. James Podmore sat glaring at the congregation. Eventually he stood up. 'Listen to what the young man is saying!'

If I could have escaped from that pulpit, I would have done so gladly. All the heads now turned towards me with one accord. I knew how Daniel felt in the lion's den. In fact, I would have preferred the lions to this rustic congregation. For the rest of the Sermon, I never raised my head, but I was aware of another 'hearty vote of thanks', this time to 'our young brother'.

During the collection, envelopes were placed on the plates. The response to the gift-day appeal lay hidden until after the service. James Podmore could not wait for the Wardens to open the envelopes. He felt each one of the brown paper containers to see whether there was a note or coins inside. After each examination, he would 'tut' for the coins, or 'ah' for the notes. There were nine 'tuts' and three 'ahs'.

'Looks better than last year,' he pronounced, 'only one note last year.'

Enter the Churchwardens and the count revealed a total of seven pounds, eleven shillings, three pence and a halfpenny. 'Two pounds, two and three up on last year,' said one of the Wardens.

'Well done, young man,' exclaimed the Vicar, slapping me on the back with a blow like a heavyweight boxer's. I smiled wanly.

An urgent necessity confronted me. I had to devise a ruse to avoid the meal at the Rectory, and its possible consequences for my stomach, not to mention my bowels. The very thought of the meal was inducing nausea.

That was it! I was feeling ill and I had to get back to my digs.

'Vicar,' I said, 'I'm afraid I am not feeling very well, I think I should get back to my digs as soon as possible. I hope you won't think I'm rude but I'm going to have to – er – miss the meal with you.'

The Reverend James Podmore looked disappointed. 'I was going to do you some home-cured ham, egg and onions,' he said, as if it were a gourmet's feast. The thought of the fat on the ham together with the onions almost precipitated a bout of sickness on the spot. 'I must say,' he added, 'you don't look very well.'

'It's kind of you to excuse me,' I said.

'Next time you must stay for a meal and taste my cooking,' said the Vicar. Then he turned to the Churchwarden. 'Have you got a cigarette, John? I've run out of smokes.'

John looked at him in a way which suggested he had answered that request on many occasions. We emerged from the vestry into the warmth of the June evening. The Vicar and his Warden lit up as I cycled off to my digs, like a condemned man who had just been given a reprieve.

'Well,' asked Mrs Richards, 'how did you get on with Mr Plodmore?'

'Having had an evening in his company,' I said, 'I shall never complain about Canon Llewellyn again. The vicarage, the Vicar and the Church were all in a filthy condition. That is the last thing you can say about Pontywen.'

'Mr Price said that everything was dirty when he went there,' replied Mrs Richards. 'Mr Plodmore is a strange man. They say that when the boiler was broken last winter he had those old farmers doing quizzical jerks. You know, "Arms up, Arms down" and that sort of thing.'

When I reported back to my Vicar next morning, I mentioned among other things his meanness in cadging cigarettes and the cheapness of his notepaper.

'Let me shock you, Secombe,' said the Canon. 'That man is one of the richest men in that part of the world. His wife was the daughter of a big quarry owner. Podmore gave her a terrible life. When her father died and left her a small fortune, she was not allowed to spend a penny of it. Podmore said he wasn't going to be a kept man. It's some years since she died but he hasn't touched a penny. Heaven knows what will happen to it when he dies.'

'Perhaps he will leave it to a home for superannuated donkeys,' I suggested.

'Don't be facetious,' said the Vicar.

11

'Bertie Owen has called,' said Mrs Richards. 'He says he hopes you don't mind but he's had to have his bike back for a few days. His engine has got to be de-coked.'

It was the Friday after the Chapter meeting and I had planned to cycle to St Illtyd's to give Mervyn Williams a Sunday off. By now, I was driving to the country church with reasonable efficiency. Mervyn seemed to think that I could manage to drive on my own – but the Vicar insisted that the lad came with me.

As it was, the Almighty took a hand and decided that the time had come for my first solo performance.

'You'll have to cycle to church tomorrow,' said my Vicar after our Saturday morning prayers. 'Mervyn Williams is in bed with tonsilitis.'

'I'm afraid I can't,' I replied. 'Bertie Owen has come for his bicycle. His car is out of commission.'

'There is only one thing for it,' said the Vicar. 'You'll have to drive on your own. Mervyn tells me that you are able to do so. So I'll have to take his word for it.'

Next day, a very anxious Vicar saw me off from the Vicarage.

'Drive carefully,' he commanded.

'Don't worry, Canon,' I said confidently, 'I can drive quite well now.'

A hundred yards up a steep road from the Vicarage, I was about to turn right on to the road to St Illtyd's. Suddenly Sir David Jones-Williams' car came round the corner on the wrong side of the road. I suppose that as he was the Squire, he considered that he had the right to drive on any part of the road he chose.

His ancient Bentley and the Canon's ancient Morris met each other and gently embraced, their bumpers locked together.

I applied the handbrake but it had retired from work. It was that old. The car began to go backwards, pulling the Bentley with it. I jammed my foot on the brake.

Lady Jones-Williams got out of the car and surveyed the scene. She was tall, thin, aristocratic, deaf and in a very bad temper.

She beat on my car window, shouting, 'Get out, man.' I was sweating profusely both from embarrassment and cramp in my right leg which was pressing on the brake.

'The brake's not working,' I said.

She did not hear me.

'Stop talking and get out,' she insisted. She opened my car door. I pointed frantically to my right foot. Whether she understood that the handbrake was not working or whether she thought I was injured in the leg, I do not know. But she shut the door.

Sir David was still behind the wheel, afraid to leave the car in case he would strangle the Curate. Fortunately, at that moment two hefty churchgoers appeared. They disentangled the bumpers and I reversed the car into the kerb which acted as a brake. An inspection of the cars revealed minor damage to the bumpers and major damage to the headlamps. In high dudgeon the Squire reversed his car and went back to his Squiredom, instead of to his church.

Completely unnerved I drove to St Illtyd's, stalling the car quite a few times on the way.

'What ever is the matter with you, Mr Secombe?' asked Miss Owen, the demon pedaller of the harmonium. 'You look quite ill, doesn't he, Tom?'

Tom Cadwallader grunted his agreement.

'It's just a headache,' I replied.

Gradually I recovered my composure as the sun poured through the dusty windows of the little church and took the chill off the stone walls. A drowsy atmosphere pervaded the sacred edifice. I was prepared for a loud sonata of snores from the Sexton.

Just before the last verse of 'Awake My Soul', I ascended the pulpit steps and opened the Bible to the tenth chapter of St Luke's Gospel, the thirtieth verse. When the congregation had collapsed into their seats, I began. 'A certain man went down from Jerusalem to Jericho.'

I waited for the first snore from Tom. It did not arrive. I went on to describe the geography of the road, what were the principal industries of Jericho and other uninteresting aspects of the journey involving the friendly old Samaritan. Still no snores.

To my amazement, when I dared to look up from my hastily written script, the Sexton was not only awake but was looking at me with wondering eyes, silent in a pew in Pontywen, if you will pardon the Keatsian phraseology. He remained like that for the rest of the sermon. I was astounded by the power of my oratory, ignoring the fact that at least two out of the other nine in the congregation were doing a 'Cadwallader'.

After the service I was disrobing in the vestry when Tom Cadwallader shambled in. He was wide awake.

'Thank you for your sermon,' he said.

'That's very kind,' I replied, not daring to ask why there were no snores.

'Well, what it is,' he continued, 'it's this. I travelled that road often.'

'You did!' I answered. It was obvious to me that either he had had a brainstorm or that senility had come prematurely. He looked as if he were only sixty at most.

'Yes,' he went on. 'I was in Palestine with Allenby.'

'Who's Allenby?' I asked.

'He was the General,' he said. 'Great man.'

Here in the heart of the countryside, was this obtuse giant of a man, a farm labourer who looked as if he had never travelled further than Cardiff. Yet he had been to places I knew only from books. It was a salutary lesson for me.

'From now on,' I said to myself. 'I will never take anybody for granted.'

After service, I got into the car and started the engine. I could not get it into gear. The men of the congregation tried pushing the car and rocking it – but to no avail.

An hour later, as I walked down the hill to the Vicarage gates, I could see the Canon standing in a cloud of tobacco smoke. From a distance, he seemed to be creating a record by smoking ten cigarettes at once.

When I reached him he was chewing the cigarette in his anxiety.

'Don't tell me,' he shouted. 'I heard the bang after you left here. I've had a phone call from Sir David. Where's the car?'

'I . . . I couldn't get it to go after the service,' I said lamely.

There was an enormous grunt.

'Go and get your dinner,' he said. 'I'll get someone to take me there.'

Next morning, at the Monday morning meeting in the Vicarage, the Vicar began by referring to my inability to start his car.

'Nothing wrong with the car,' he snorted. 'I got it into gear right away.'

As he said that, the light dawned on me; I had been putting my foot on the brake instead of the clutch, as those brawny farmers were pushing. I kept silent.

That was the end of my driving at Pontywen. It was Bertie Owen's bicycle from then on.

However, I did have a ride in a car to St Illtyd's one week later. Emily Humphries, eighty-six years of age, spinster of that parish, passed away peacefully in her sleep. It was decided to hold the funeral on Monday afternoon to avoid clashing with the opening of the rugby season on Saturday.

Very rarely did Tom Cadwallader have to dig a grave. The population around St Illtyd's was sparse and the air up in the hills was like wine.

On Sunday evening when I took service at the church, Tom's normally expressionless face wore a frown. His snores were perfunctory and muted. Something was wrong. He came into the vestry after Evensong, evidently greatly concerned about something.

'You taking the service tomorrow?' he asked.

'Yes,' I said. 'The Canon has got to go to the Cathedral for a meeting.'

'I haven't finished the grave,' he replied. 'Blessed rock,' he added.

He may have 'blessed' the rock to me but I expect he had another version for anyone else.

'I would have thought that with your strength you would get through anything,' I said.

He looked hurt.

'Can't get through rock with a shovel,' he grunted. 'Not even with a pick.'

Monday afternoon I arrived at the church in style in the front seat of the limousine belonging to Obadiah Evans and Son, Undertakers, Cardiff. As I dismounted, through the door, opened by the son of Obadiah, I could see Tom Cadwallader in the churchyard, leaning on a pick and gazing into the open grave.

The cortège of black-clad mourners moved into church, led by myself reciting the burial sentence, closely followed by Obadiah junior with doffed top hat and a black suit which could have served for a Buckingham Palace garden party. Miss Owen, the organist, was playing Handel's 'Largo' in a manner more insulting to the great composer than complimentary.

There were about twenty mourners present, all dry-eyed, with the front pew's occupants evidently more concerned

117

about the reading of the will than their parting from the bereaved.

I was reading from St Paul, 'For the trumpet shall sound and the dead shall be raised incorruptible . . .' All of a sudden, there was a loud explosion outside. It appeared that the Day of Judgement had arrived.

Obadiah Junior rushed out of church followed by his four minions. I carried on with One Corinthians Fifteen despite the fact that twenty heads were turned towards the back of the church instead of towards me. I got through the prayers and began the final hymn without a sign of the professionals.

Just before the end of 'Nearer my God to Thee', they re-appeared, showing signs of unbecoming hilarity. By the time the organist had moved on to the 'Dead March in Saul', they had regained their composure.

We emerged from the church into the open air. One could hardly describe it as fresh air. It was too full of cordite for that.

Waiting at the graveside with a face which looked as if it had been down a coal mine and wearing a somewhat startled expression was Tom Cadwallader. As we approached the last resting place for Emily Humphries, there was no doubt that she was about to be buried in a crater rather than a grave. Pieces of rock were scattered around the hole in the ground. A nearby gravestone had keeled over while another was drunkenly aslant.

With great difficulty the four Cardiff experts lowered the coffin into the shell hole. Judging by the size of the excavation, it would take the Sexton a fortnight to fill it in.

When the mourners had left, I went over to Tom who had been hiding behind a yew tree. He looked distinctly sheepish.

'What happened, Tom?' I asked.

Out came the longest string of sentences I had heard from him.

'I went to the Quarry for some dynamite. You'd still be waiting otherwise. I used too much.'

12

'Let us pray for the Church here . . .' Before I could say any more of the prayer, I was startled by a loud hiss, like that of an escaped cobra.

It was the Wednesday after the explosive burial and I was standing at the altar in the Parish Church with my back to the congregation. I decided to ignore the interruption. The next few sentences were punctuated by a series of hisses, growing in intensity.

Something serious has happened, I said to myself. I suspended operations and turned around. There was Full-Back in all his glory, battered trilby on his head, filthy raincoat and wellies to complete the outfit. He was frantically indicating with his thumb that he wanted to see me in the vestry.

To the consternation of the six godly ladies who formed the congregation, I made a hurried exit from the altar and pushed him inside the vestry.

'What's happened?' I asked breathlessly.

A sheepish, toothless grin appeared on his face. 'Can I borrow the Church ladder to put some slates on my roof?' he said.

I exploded. 'What do you think you are doing? Can't you see I'm taking a service?'

He looked hurt. 'Sorry, Boss,' he said. 'I thought you was talking to yourself. I didn't know there was anybody in the auditorium.'

'For heaven's sake take the church ladder and go,' I said. 'I've had enough trouble with gravediggers this week!'

'What do you mean, Boss?' He looked puzzled.

'Just go – will you?' I said between gritted teeth and gave him a not so gentle push out through the vestry door.

When I came back into church, Mrs Llewellyn and the other five ladies had given up their devotions and they were standing in a little gossip circle in the middle of the aisle. Evidently the Vicar's wife was delivering a lecture on the excesses of gravediggers.

'I must apologise for the interruption,' I announced. The sight of the knot of scandal-mongers who should have been on their knees made me add, 'Normal service will now be resumed.'

Mrs Llewellyn's eyebrows shot up to the heavens, and then knitted themselves together. Trouble was brewing, it was plain.

After the service, the Vicar's wife stormed into the vestry.

'What was the reason for Jones' disgraceful behaviour?' she demanded.

'Apparently he hadn't realised that a service was going on,' I said.

'In that case, he must be blind and deaf,' she snorted. 'And what did he want?'

'He wanted to borrow the ladder to see to some slates on his roof,' I replied.

'Well, that's it,' she decided. 'He's got to go. And as for you with your flippant remark about "normal service", that was quite unpardonable.'

'I'm sorry, Mrs Llewellyn.' I could feel my temper rising. 'It was something which came from my subconscious.'

'I don't know where it came from, but it should have stayed where it was,' she said acidly.

The Vicar was away for a few days attending committee meetings of various kinds. In his absence, it was obvious Mrs Llewellyn felt she was in charge of the shop. I was determined to show her that she had no right to be in charge.

'As I say,' I found it difficult to control my words, 'I am sorry you found my remark offensive. It was partly provoked by seeing worshippers standing in the aisle talking, when they should have been on their knees in the pews. As for Full-Back Jones, surely the Vicar is the person to make any decision about him.'

I had once been told by a long-suffering Curate, that the female of Vicar is Vixen. The torrent of abuse which poured over me as a result of my words justified that title for Mrs Llewellyn. She unfolded a list of complaints about me from incompetence in the pulpit and the Vicar's car to a charge of wilful damage to her leather shopping bag.

Picking up my suitcase with a flourish, I said, 'I am going. Good morning, Mrs Llewellyn.'

As I swung the receptacle from the desk, it flew open and my robes were scattered over the floor. I felt an urge to burst into laughter until I saw the scowling face looking down at me, as I knelt to recover my belongings.

'Typical,' she said with a sneer and made the grand exit I had planned for myself.

The next day, I was due at the Vicarage for the delayed weekly 'business meeting' caused by the Vicar's absence. I was expecting to be hauled over the coals – perhaps 'dragged' would be a more appropriate word.

In the event, it turned out quite differently. The Vicar met me at the door instead of Mrs Llewellyn. He did not appear to be irate.

'I gather that the gravediggers have been troublesome while I have been away,' he grunted, once he had settled himself in his seat of power behind the desk.

'I'm afraid they have,' I said nervously. 'Tom Cadwallader has caused – er – some damage to a couple of graves. I think Full-Back made a genuine error yesterday. He didn't realise he was interrupting a service.'

The Vicar put his head on one side and closed his right eye – a sure indication that a pronouncement was to follow. 'Cadwallader acted very irresponsibly – very. Fortunately there are few burials at St Illtyds. As for Jones, I take your word for it that the idiot thought you were on your own.'

Then he frowned. 'There's just one thing, young man. Don't be flippant at the altar.'

That was all – no word about my altercation with Mrs Llewellyn. I began to warm to him . . .

After I mumbled an apology, he continued, 'The Bishop has asked me to take another Curate. Apparently he is lacking in self-confidence and has only been ordained a few weeks. His Vicar asked his lordship if he could get rid of him. I am getting too old for this sort of thing.'

It was the first time he had treated me as a confidante. I felt flattered.

The doorbell rang.

'Will you go to the door, Secombe?' said the Vicar. 'Mrs Llewellyn is out. I expect it is the prospective Curate.'

When I opened the door, the long-haired figure standing before me was more like a prospective replacement for Full-Back. He was wearing a brown jacket with holes at the elbow, half-covered with leather patches which were giving up the struggle to hide them. His grey flannel trousers were in need of a clean while his red pullover was decorated with the remains of yesterday's dinner. The clerical collar looked out of place as part of the ensemble.

'My name is Wentworth-Baxter,' he announced, with as much aplomb as if he were a member of the House of Lords.

'The Vicar is expecting you,' I said. 'My name is Secombe and I am the Curate here.'

I put out my hand to shake his but he stalked past me.

'The Vicar is in here,' I said and ushered the hyphenated gentleman into the study. The Vicar's eyebrows were raised as high as Mrs Llewellyn's the previous morning.

'Sit down,' ordered the Vicar, indicating the empty chair opposite mine.

Wentworth-Baxter dipped into the pocket of his scruffy jacket and produced a packet of Woodbines.

'Do you mind if I smoke?' he asked. It sounded more like a challenge than a polite request.

'Yes I do,' the Vicar snapped, as if tobacco had never polluted his lips.

The packet went back hastily into the jacket pocket.

'Now then, the Bishop says you are unhappy in your present parish even though you have been there just a few weeks. It seems you would like to come here.'

'I thought it was definite,' replied the Reverend Wentworth-Baxter.

The Vicar's temper shot up to boiling point.

'Bishop or no Bishop,' he roared, 'if I think I can do nothing with you, you are *not* coming here.'

The effect on Wentworth-Baxter was electric. He seemed to shrink into a dwarf. It was obvious that he had a large inferiority complex.

'My apologies,' he stammered.

I felt sorry for the young man. He was looking like a frightened puppy.

'There are a number of conditions I shall impose if you come here.' The Vicar's tone had softened already. 'First, you must get that hair cut. Second, you are not to go around the parish looking like a tramp. Have you a dark suit?'

'Yes, Vicar,' he said meekly. 'That's the only other suit I have.'

'Well, keep wearing it until you can get another,' commanded my superior.

On the Saturday of the following week, he arrived in the parish. The Vicar had arranged for him to stay with Mrs Powell alias Betsy Trotwood. This was to ensure that he was kept in order. The Vicar had also arranged that he would come to St Padarn's with me for the Harvest Thanksgiving Service on Sunday morning. He was to preach and I was to look after him.

Saturday brought the usual chaos, called 'decorating the church for Harvest'. Ladies were colliding with each other as they fought to get water from the tap in the vestry. They fought each other for the best flowers for their particular part of the church. The older ladies had had their own patch since the tin church had been erected forty years ago.

Mrs Partridge 'did' the lectern which always featured two bunches of grapes hanging down from either side. She was over eighty years old, deaf and short-sighted but she was first in church to see that no one invaded her preserve. The only lady, a newcomer, who ever attempted to help Mrs P. went home with a nervous breakdown.

In the middle of the confusion was Bertie Owen, out of his element, because it was the ladies' day. Without his sidesmen, he was like a general without troops. As far as I could see, his sole contribution to the decoration was a tumbler of water on the ledge of the pulpit.

'It's a dual-purpose tumbler, Mr Secombe,' explained Bertie. 'It shows our gratitude to God for water and it can help the preacher if his throat is dry.'

'I'm sure the new Curate will be very grateful for the water if his mouth gets dry through nervousness,' I said.

'Oh, the new man will be preaching, will he?' enquired Bertie.

On cue, entered the Reverend Wentworth-Baxter, mark two. Someone had placed a pudding basin on his head and cut off whatever was hanging underneath. He was wearing a black suit, with a liberal amount of stains on his waistcoat and jacket. It appeared that the razor had not touched his face since the previous day. He looked as if he had just risen from his bed.

'Here he is,' I announced.

Bertie's jaw dropped.

'I thought I would come and have a look at the church before I preach tomorrow,' said the new Curate.

'This is Mr Bertie Owen, the Churchwarden,' I said.

'Pleased to meet you,' said Bertie, offering his hand.

'How d'you do,' replied Wentworth-Baxter, offering a few fingers in return. 'I didn't realise this was a tin church. In need of a lick of paint, isn't it?'

Bertie flushed. 'Don't forget there's been a war on,' he said.

'I think you'll find it isn't the building that makes a church but the people in it,' I commented frostily.

'Hear! hear!' trumpeted Bertie loudly, startling the decorators.

'Would you like to come and have a cup of tea at my digs?' I asked my new colleague. I thought it would be advisable to remove him before he made any more tactless remarks.

'I'd love to,' he replied, to my surprise. 'By the way, I'm Charles.'

'I'm Fred.' We shook hands for the first time.

He stayed at my digs for a couple of hours. It transpired that he had taken a second at Oxford in theology. His father was an elderly clergyman from Gloucestershire who had settled in the Welsh countryside and had insisted that his son followed in his footsteps. Charles had done so reluctantly.

Before he left, I reminded him that the clocks went back that night. He seemed to be the kind of person who needed that reminder.

'He's a nice young man,' was Mrs Richards' judgement, 'but he looks a bit of a crackerbrain.'

'I'm afraid he is,' I replied.

Next morning I had just begun my ablutions when there was a banging on the front door. Mrs Richards was still in bed. By now I had insisted on boiling my shaving water to allow the old lady a longer rest. With a face half smothered in shaving soap, I dashed downstairs to discover what crisis had arisen.

On the doorstep was Charles Wentworth-Baxter in a state of great perturbation.

'There's no one there,' he said, breathlessly.

'Where?' I asked.

'In church,' he replied.

'Of course not,' I said testily. 'There's another hour and a half before service.'

'But the clocks!' he breathed. 'They are altered today, aren't they?'

I could see only too plainly why his Vicar had got rid of him.

'They were put back, not forward,' I said between closed teeth.

He stared at me for a moment.

'Oh!' he said.

'Yes – oh!' I replied. 'You had better get back to the house and read over your sermon or something useful like that.'

An hour later, I made my way to the church. As I opened the vestry door, the smell of fruit and flowers assailed my nostrils. There is nothing like a harvest festival for smells. It is a veritable symphony for the nose.

I went into the sanctuary to prepare for the service. As I made my way past the foliage inside the sanctuary, carrying the wine and water to the table at the side, I trod on something on the floor. I looked down. There was the announcement 'God is Love' – a work of art, made up of small biscuits.

Admittedly that text is probably the most important in the Bible. However, there is a place for everything and biscuits are not a suitable medium for Biblical texts. I stormed into the vestry. The new Curate had just arrived.

'Who on earth put biscuits on the floor of the sanctuary?' I demanded.

The half of the choir who had arrived, stared at me as if I were mad.

Charles Wentworth-Baxter dropped his head.

'You didn't?' I said incredulously.

'There was a packet of biscuits in the chancel when I came here this morning,' he mumbled 'and I thought it would be nice to use them like that.'

A giggle spread through the choristers' ranks. Before long, I could see, Charles Wentworth-Baxter would be known as a 'proper Charlie'. I suppressed an urge to join in the merriment and led him aside.

'Don't do that again,' I said, controlling myself with difficulty. 'Now then,' I added, 'you will give out the hymns, read the lesson and preach. I will make the announcements and take the service.'

When we went into the church, I made all the announcements and finished by welcoming the new curate into the parish. He sat there beaming. I waited for him to get up and announce the hymn. He still sat there grinning like a Cheshire cat. I pointed up to the hymn board. He looked at it and then looked back at me. I gave up.

'Hymn number three hundred and eighty-two,' I announced finally.

As the hymn was being sung, I went over to him.

'You are supposed to announce the hymns,' I said. Exasperation was setting in rapidly.

'Sorry,' he replied. 'I'll watch you to see when I do it.'

He did that. He never took his eyes off me.

After the prayers, I pointed to the hymn board. He arose and announced the hymn we had already sung. The choir was in danger of becoming hysterical. Once again I had to announce the hymn. Once again I went over to him.

'You now read the lesson,' I said as calmly as I could. 'I will announce the hymns for the rest of the service.'

I went back to my stall. Charles went to the lectern.'

The lesson had been turned up for him to read. For some strange reason he decided to turn over a page to see what was on the other side.

Mrs Partridge's grapes on the left-hand side became entangled with his surplice. In his attempt to prevent them disappearing up his sleeve, he dislodged them and they fell into a sheaf of corn. Instead of ignoring the accident, he proceeded to come down from the platform. The hymn before the lesson ended and he was still there underneath the lectern picking up the grapes.

'Leave them and read the lesson!' I shouted from my stall.

The choir and congregation were convulsed. It was better than any show they had seen in the church hall.

I have never heard a lesson read so badly as his rendition of Deuteronomy, chapter eight. However, he managed to leave the lectern without falling over, as I thought might happen.

For that I was profoundly grateful.

As the Creed began I went across to him for the fourth time to the great amusement of all present.

'This is where you preach your sermon,' I said.

He flopped to his knees. Whether he was asking for Divine guidance for his sermon or for an end to all his embarrassments, I do not know. Whatever it was, his prayers were not answered.

The Reverend Charles Wentworth-Baxter made his way to the pulpit. He produced his sermon from his cassock and proceeded to place it on the little reading desk on the pulpit.

The Curate began his sermon by reading his first two pages without any sign of animation. On page three he felt moved to express his feelings with a gesture. His right hand was used to drive home a point and Bertie Owen's tumbler of water found a third purpose. It showered upon Mrs Annie Jones and Mrs Collier in the front pew and crashed into smithereens at the foot of the pulpit.

This was the signal for Bertie Owen to dart into the vestry and emerge with a towel. He dashed down the aisle to the aid of the ladies while they were mopping their faces, stood at their side, semaphoring to me that there were ninety-seven people for communion.

In the meantime, a red-faced Charles Wentworth-Baxter, with his head bent over his notes, was delivering a sermon to a congregation who were trying to cope with hysterics. Idris the Milk was doing his best to subdue himself as well as the male members of the choir, with little success. The only two who were not amused were Mrs Jones and Mrs Collier.

The climax to this harvest farce came when Bertie, having returned to the vestry with the towel, proceeded to walk down the aisle with a sweeping brush to deal with the broken glass. If the new Curate had any sense, he would have finished his sermon abruptly and come down from the pulpit. Unfortunately since he was devoid of that commodity, he continued with his very erudite address which was more suitable for a lecture room than St Padarn's.

I decided the time had come for action on my part. I came out from my stall and met Bertie at the foot of the pulpit.

'Get back to the vestry with that,' I whispered. Bertie looked hurt.

'You can't leave that broken glass there with people coming for communion,' he said loudly.

'You can leave it there until the sermon is finished,' I insisted.

He retreated into the vestry while the congregation

watched his progress with unconcealed glee, waiting for the next circus act.

Still Charles Wentworth-Baxter droned on with his nose a few inches away from his script. As I was debating whether I should get him down, the preacher said, 'I can only hope that what I have said has demonstrated the limitations of Pelagianism and emphasised the boundless nature of divine providence. Amen.'

'Amen,' intoned Bertie Owen fervently. The next second he was sprinting down the aisle, brush in one hand and dustpan in the other. Unfortunately, he was so intent on his mission, that he did not see the new Curate who, with head bent to hide his blushes, had made his way down from the pulpit. It was a head on collision. The crack could be heard at the back of the church.

Broom and dustpan went flying as Bertie collapsed into the lap of Annie Jones. She was just about to put her teeth in for the next hymn. The teeth shot into the air and landed on Charles Wentworth-Baxter who lay at the foot of the pulpit, his body decorated with the pages of his sermon.

It took several minutes to revive the injured and even longer to restore calm to the hysterical congregation.

'St Padarn's will never be the same again, mun,' commented Idris the Milk afterwards. 'We had more laughs than watching Laurel and Hardy.'

'Come to think of it,' I said, 'if Charles and Bertie teamed up, they'd make a fortune.'

'Well, as they do say,' replied Idris, 'Hollywood's loss is Pontywen's gain.'

'I don't think the Vicar will see it that way,' I thought to myself.

13

'I can't stand much more. It's like living in Colditz. 'Charles W–B had been incarcerated with Mrs Powell for just a week.

We were in my room where he had come for refuge. 'Look how lovely your place is. There is a warmth here. That front parlour where she has dumped me is like a morgue, with pictures of her dead husband staring at me every time I sit down. I get the feeling he resents my presence.' He paused and then launched into a catalogue of complaints.

'She sounds exactly like my college landlady,' I said. 'The only thing you can do is to tell the Vicar at our Monday morning get-together that you want to move from there.'

'It's easy to say that,' said Charles 'but what's the Vicar going to think of me. I was only a few weeks in my last parish and now I want to leave my lodgings here after a week.'

'In a sense it's the Vicar's fault,' I said. 'He should have known what life would be like with Mrs Powell. Perhaps he will be more sympathetic than you think. The best plan is to find an alternative place and to suggest that to our Lord and Master.'

'How on earth am I going to do that?' he asked. 'In any case, he'll think I am interfering with his arrangements.'

'I'll make discreet enquiries at St Padarn's tomorrow while you're keeping the Vicar company at the parish church.'

'That's another thing,' moaned Charles. 'I hope I don't make such a mess of things as I did last Sunday.'

'For heaven's sake, man,' I exclaimed, 'snap out of it. Everybody's first Sunday in a new parish is an ordeal. Mine wasn't exactly a great success.'

'Wasn't it?' he asked, brightening up.

'It certainly wasn't. I got mixed up about the hymns, just

like you. Maybe I didn't drown the ladies in the front row, but then there was no glass of water on the pulpit ledge.'

He laughed for the first time for days.

Next morning I had a word with Idris about Charles' dilemma.

'The only person I can think of offhand,' said the milkman, 'is Annie Jones. She's got a spare room.'

'Quite frankly, I don't think that would be a wise move. She tends to be too friendly to curates.'

'It won't be long before her old man is back from the forces, Mr Secombe. He's been abroad for years. She's telling everybody he's being demobbed, so I wouldn't worry about that side of things.'

'Anyway if you can think of anybody else before tomorrow, Idris, I'd be grateful.'

'I'll put my thinking-cap on,' he said.

During Sunday dinner I asked Mrs Richards whether she knew of any likely landlady for my hapless colleague.

'He hasn't been here two shakes of a dead sheep's tail and he wants to move already,' she said severely.

'You must admit, Mrs Richards, that his present landlady is hardly the kind of person to mother a young man who is lacking in confidence.'

'Who's a crackerbrain, you mean.'

'All right, who's a crackerbrain.' She was broadening my vocabulary every day.

'I suppose you're right,' she admitted and paused in thought. 'Moelwyn the fruiterer has got a couple of rooms to spare. They used to have those vacuums from London. Myfanwy, his wife, is very clean, spotless, but quite homely. There's only one fly in the box of ointment . . .'

'What's that?'

'Well, Myfanwy is a nonconformist, Baptist. Moelwyn is church, of course.'

'I didn't know he's a churchman.'

'Oh yes. He gives to anything for the church and he comes for the big festivities like Christmas or Easter. His father was very regular – every Sunday.'

'Perhaps I'll call round there after Sunday school,' I said.

*   *   *

Sunday school was a constant source of entertainment. Matthew Morris and his brother, Ben, were still attending every Sunday – unwashed and smelly. Matthew's duels with Captain Eynon's son, David, always brightened the day for me – until that very afternoon.

Invariably, the two brothers were first at the tin church, waiting for the doors to open, as if it were a cinema. True to form, they were there when I arrived. Matthew was not as chirpy as usual and Ben was fretful.

As the benches began to fill, young Eynon strutted in with a self-satisfied grin on his countenance. Tommy Harris seated himself by his best friend, Matthew.

We sang the first hymn and I said prayers. Then the Sunday school split up into classes.

As soon as I sat down to mark the register for my class, I could see that something was wrong.

David Eynon could scarcely contain himself, as he waited to pass on some news. When I finished the roll-call, he burst forth with his information.

'Please sir, Matthew Morris's father is a deserter and the red caps have been to look for him at his house.'

Matthew hurled himself at Eynon and seized him by the throat. I had to move in quickly to prevent strangulation.

'David Eynon,' I said, after parting the two, 'if you come to Sunday school and tell tales like that any more I shall have to ask you to leave.'

For the next twenty minutes, while I talked about St Catherine of Alexandria and her martyrdom on a wheel of knives, I had complete attention from all the bloodthirsty boys, except Matthew who glowered throughout.

At the end of the lessons, the Sunday School came together for my weekly talk. Matthew was joined by his little brother, the two sitting close together for mutual comfort.

I had chosen the story of Androcles and the lion for my address. The story was going down very well with an attentive audience.

Suddenly, Matthew stood up and pulled Ben with him, pushing the boys aside as he made for the aisle.

'What do you want, Matthew?' I asked.

'Can I take 'im to the lav'?' he demanded.

'Yes, go on,' I said, 'you know where it is. Through that door at the back.'

He caused the maximum disruption as he dragged his brother with him to the lavatory, banging the door shut as he went inside.

When everybody settled down, I strove to recapture the attention I had won, prior to Matthew's disturbance. By dint of some intense ham acting, I got my audience interested again. I warmed to my task. There was an expectant hush as I reached that part of the story when the lion was about to pounce on Androcles – before he recognised him as the Good Samaritan, who had taken the thorn out of his paw. I was crouching with my arms extended in imitation of the lion.

The door at the back crashed open. Matthew emerged as every head switched from me to him. 'Hey,' he shouted. 'There's no paper in this lav'. This is an 'opeless church.'

One of the women teachers quickly reached the door at the back with some scribbling paper. Matthew snatched it and slammed the door.

My address was ruined. I called it a day and announced the last hymn. Before the hymn had ended, Matthew and Ben had left the church. They never returned.

As I was locking up the church, Idris the Milk appeared.

'I've been thinking about "digs" for the new Curate,' he said. 'Moelwyn the fruit and his missis have got accommodation.'

'All great minds think alike,' I replied. 'They are the very people Mrs Richards suggested. So it must be the place for Charles W–B. I think I'll go and see them now before tea.'

'Mind you,' said Idris, 'I don't think the Vicar will like all this going on behind his back. You know what 'e's like.'

'So far, the only people who know that Charles wants a change of address are you, me and Mrs Richards. With a bit of luck and a favouring wind, perhaps something will turn up to convince the Vicar that an immediate change is needed.' With these words, I hurried to the fruiterer's shop.

Moelwyn's military moustache twitched as much at my enquiry about accommodation for my colleague as it had when confronted with the law in the police box some weeks before.

'Well, we have got rooms here, but I don't know whether it is suitable for a Curate to live over a fruit and veg shop. It's true, we've got a side entrance, which people could use if they wanted to see him.' Moelwyn turned to his wife. 'What do you think, love?'

Myfanwy Howells, grey haired and plump, was a jolly person, invariably smiling. 'As far as I am concerned, Moelwyn,' she said, 'he can come here with pleasure. The only thing is that I'm not church but I don't think that's any reason for him not to come here.'

'Are you agreed then, that if we get the Vicar's permission, he can come?' I asked.

The moustache twitched once more. Moelwyn looked at his wife who gave her silent approval and then looked at me as if he had come to a momentous decision.

'Done,' he pronounced and shook my hand firmly.

'I'd be grateful if you said nothing until we see whether my friend is allowed to leave his lodgings,' I said.

'Not another word,'replied Moelwyn. 'Have some of my parsnip wine before you go.'

He poured me a tumblerful. I sat for ten minutes drinking the delicious liquid and then made my way out into late afternoon sunlight.

The fresh air had a strange effect on my legs. They seemed to be in competition with each other. Suddenly an alarm bell rang in my head. I remembered the story about my grandfather's parsnip wine rendering the local curate drunk and incapable. Here I was – about to take a service at St Padarn's in an hour or so's time.

'At least my head is clear, even if my legs won't co-operate,' I told myself.

I reached thirteen Mount Pleasant View without falling – a remarkable feat, since my legs seemed to be in a state of constant collision.

As I opened the door, a worried Mrs Richards met me. 'There's a man in your room waiting to see you. Calls himself Captain Eynon,' she whispered. 'He's very aggravated.'

'So am I,' I said. 'I've had some parsnip wine so he had better look out.'

Captain Eynon was a short, pot-bellied man with a black

moustache and horn-rimmed glasses. His face was red with anger. He was standing in front of the fireplace.

'What's this about David being attacked by a deserter's son from Maes-y-Coed Avenue?' The street had a bad name and a sneer was implicit in his tone as he pronounced it.

'I think, Mr Eynon,' he winced at the 'mister', 'I think your boy deserved what he got. He was not hurt. I stopped the "attack" before any injury could be done. No child wants to hear that his father is a deserter – especially when another boy glories in telling the whole class as your David did.'

The 'Captain' looked as if he was on the verge of attacking me but restrained himself at the last second.

'You—you whippersnapper,' he snarled. 'You should have been serving your king and country instead of skulking behind that collar.'

'That collar, as you call it,' I said indignantly, 'was not provided to shield me from conscription. I was a theological student before war broke out. We were advised to carry on with our studies ready for ordination. Since then I have been an air-raid warden, firewatcher and a member of the Royal Observer Corps. What active service have you seen?'

His temperature dropped rapidly. He swallowed hard.

'Unfortunately, I have very bad eyesight and failed to get into the Forces. Instead I did the best I could and rose to the rank of Captain in the Home Guard. But, believe me, if I had been fit, I would have been out there fighting.'

'Instead, you have spent the war years in Pontywen,' I said. 'You have not seen a single bomb drop in this place. Yet you have the cheek to talk about Matthew Morris as "A deserter's son!" For all you know, that man might have had a bellyful of real active service.'

Emboldened by the parsnip wine, I was beginning to enjoy the experience of putting down 'Captain' Eynon.

The enjoyment was cut short. My visitor moved towards the door.'I can't stay any longer swapping insults with you. All I can tell you is that David will no longer be coming to Sunday school. Goodbye, Padre.'

'That's up to you,' I said. 'Goodbye, Mr Eynon.'

As he left, Mrs Richards came out of the middle room.

'I heard a lot of shouting, Mr Secombe. Is everything all right?'

'Fine,' I replied. 'It did me a lot of good. I hope it did him some too.'

'I'm glad,' she said. 'All's well when it ends well.'

After service, Charles came round to plan some kind of joint strategy for the meeting at the Vicarage next morning.

'I've found a place for you – very nice people. Moelwyn and Myfanwy Howells – the fruiterers. That's if you want to go there.'

'Wherever it is, it will be better than where I am now.' Charles looked very depressed.

'I had trouble with giving out the hymns again this evening,' he added. 'I looked at the wrong list on my desk and announced the hymn from the morning service, and there were one or two other things. I don't think the Vicar will be in the right frame of mind tomorrow to agree to a change of "digs".'

He did not specify the 'one or two other things'. I could imagine the scene in any case. Tomorrow appeared to be a most unpromising time for Charles to request anything.

Mrs Richards made us some bubble and squeak out of the remains of our Sunday dinner. We listened to the nine o'clock news on my newly acquired second-hand wireless set and then talked for a while. Charles seemed much more relaxed.

'I'd better go now,' he said. 'What's the time?'

I looked at my watch. It was ten o'clock.

He ran through the door like a frightened rabbit. 'See you in the morning,' I shouted as he sprinted down the street.

'I feel sorry for that young crackerbrain,' said Mrs Richards as she cleared away our plates. 'I hope he can get in with the Howellses. That Mrs Powell is far too dominating for him. Mind, it's the Vicar who's going to be the tumbling-block. How the Curate is going to get round that, I don't know.'

There was a loud knock at the door.

'It's nearly half past ten,' said Mrs Richards, startled out of her wits. 'You'd better go and see who it is this time of the night.'

On the doorstep was my colleague, as white as a sheet.

'Come on in, for heaven's sake,' I said.

He sat down in my armchair, still breathless from running.

'It's that woman,' he gasped. 'She's locked me out. I've banged on the front door. I've climbed over the wall at the back to see if I could get in through the back door but that's locked of course. What am I going to do?'

'Calm down Charles.' I patted him on the shoulder. 'There are only two alternatives. One is to break in and risk the attentions of Will Book and Pencil, not to mention Mrs Powell. The other is to spend the night here. That is the obvious solution. Stay there and I'll see Mrs Richards.

I went into the middle room. The old lady was looking perturbed.

'Don't worry,' I reassured her. 'It's only Charles. Mrs Powell has locked him out.'

'The old handbag!' exclaimed my landlady. It was the only time I ever heard her come near to swearing.

'Would you mind if he spent the night here?'

'Certainly not,' she said. 'I'll bring a blanket down from upstairs. He can sleep in your armchair. He'll be as snug as a bug with a rug.'

'Thank you, Mrs Richards,' I replied. 'You're a very kind lady.'

'It's only what anyone else would do.' She was flattered by my remark. 'I'll bring you both a cup of tea. I expect Mr Baxton will need it.'

When I came back into my room, Charles' colour was beginning to come back.

'Mrs Richards will be delighted to have you as a guest for tonight,' I announced. 'She said you can have my armchair and a blanket. What's more, she's bringing us both a cup of tea.'

He brightened up considerably.

'You realise what this means,' I said to him.

'What does it mean?' he asked, 'except one hell of a row with Mrs Powell tomorrow.'

'It means, you slow of understanding young gentleman, that you have been given a very stong case to put before the Vicar tomorrow. This is 1945 not 1845. You are not in a prison, neither are you in some kind of boarding school. You are twenty-three years of age, a responsible adult. You cannot possibly be expected to stay in lodgings where you are locked out because you have returned after half past nine.'

'Do you think the Vicar will see it like that?'

'Of course he will.' I could see that light was dawning on him. He was indeed slow of understanding.

'As far as I can see,' I continued, 'the only difficulty is to suggest that you stay at Moelwyn's without giving the impression that something has already been done about it. That is going to be my task.'

'It's that or the dole queue.'

By the time I had placed my head on my pillow, my optimism about Charles' prospects had evaporated. Canon R.S.T. Llewellyn was not one to be hoodwinked, even by an experienced hoodwinker – let along a novice like me. I racked my brain for ingenious ploys. Wearied by the impossible, it became numb and the nirvana of sleep descended upon me.

At two twenty-five a.m., by my pocket watch, I was rudely awakened by the clatter of an overturned bucket and a loud unclerical oath. Charles was attempting to find the outside lavatory, in pitch darkness.

I opened my bedroom window, 'Why don't you put the light on in the scullery?' I hissed.

'I don't want to wake anybody,' he said.

'You amaze me,' I snarled and closed the window.

It was another hour before I could get back to nirvana. However, that must have been unknown territory to my hapless colleague.

14

'I must do something about that bathroom,' said Mrs Richards to me as Charles W–B was closeted in there using my shaving soap and safety razor. 'It needs a flick of paint.'

'Don't worry,' I reassured her, 'Charles is far too concerned about the meeting at the vicarage this morning to notice the state of the bathroom. I think he has been awake all night.'

This was borne out when he came down to breakfast. His face was wounded in a number of places and bore a fearful scowl.

'The condemned man is not about to eat a hearty breakfast,' I said cheerfully.

The scowl intensified.

'Mind you don't turn the milk off,' I continued. 'It's bad for the cornflakes. If you go to the vicarage looking like that you can forget any idea about changing your digs.'

'Shut up, you idiot,' he snapped. 'It's all right for you to be chirpy. You are not in my place.'

He toyed with the cornflakes, refused the offer of a boiled egg and then proceeded to smoke half a dozen Woodbines at a rate of knots. By the time we left for the vicarage, my room smelt like the saloon bar of the Lamb and Flag at closing time.

'Do you think you ought to call in at Mother Powell's on the way?' I asked him.

'Not on your nellie,' he snorted. 'It's enough to have to face the Vicar, let alone that old monster.'

We arrived on the vicarage doorstep, prompt at ten o'clock. Mrs Llewellyn confronted us when we rang the bell. She liked Charles W–B even less than she did me.

'The Canon is waiting for you in the study.' This was said

with a dead-pan face, like a butler addressing those who should have been at the tradesmen's entrance.

As we entered the study, the Vicar stubbed out half a cigarette hurriedly. Charles reached for his Woodbines automatically and replaced them in his pocket as quickly as he had produced them. It was going to be a morning fraught with tension.

We sat in the leather armchairs which, as usual, smelt of furniture polish, very recently applied.

'Before you say anything,' said the vicar, addressing Charles, and looking like a judge about to deliver sentence, 'I think you should know that Mrs Powell has been here to see me.'

My junior colleague jerked upright, as if the armchair was electrified.

'Before Charles says anything,' I interjected, 'I think you should know, Vicar, that he spent the night at my digs. He was locked out at ten o'clock last night, after returning from an evening with me.'

'Secombe,' thundered the Vicar, 'will you please let the young man speak for himself?'

The 'young man' began his defence with a stammering tongue. 'It's – er – true, sir, that I was with Fred last night. I – er – tried to get into the house on – er – my return. I banged on the door several times. I climbed the wall at the back but the scullery door was locked. So the only thing to do was to go back to Mount Pleasant View. But can I say something else?' Charles was getting into his stride.

'Carry on,' grunted the Vicar.

'I have only been there a week but it has already become quite unbearable: I am underfed; I have no heating in my room; worst of all, I am treated like an inmate of a concentration camp. I realise that my stay in my last parish was only a matter of weeks, but I must tell you, Vicar, that if you insist that I stay with that woman, I shall have to resign – even if it means having to leave the ministry.'

It was quite a *tour de force* and I felt tempted to applaud. The Vicar's face was a study. He had been all set to shoot down Charles in flames. This violent counter-attack caught him unawares. His one eye was closed in thought while his other little eye studied the floor. He spent some seconds in heavy breathing.

'Well, young man,' he said ultimately. 'I didn't realise the extent of your tribulations. You don't have to resign. We shall have to find somewhere else for you.'

I jumped in quickly. 'Excuse me, Vicar,' I said in my best deferential tone, 'I hope you don't think I am interfering once again but I happen to know that Moelwyn Howells and his wife have rooms where Charles could stay.'

The Vicar looked me in the eye.

'You mean you have asked them?' he said.

'I made some polite enquiries yesterday,' I replied cautiously.

'Next time you make "polite enquiries", let me know first,' he said. It was a much milder rebuke than I expected. Addressing Charles, he continued. 'Perhaps you had better see Mr and Mrs Howells later today. If the lodgings are suitable, then the sooner you move from Mrs Powell's house, the better. I think we had both better have a word with her. Whatever happens, young man, you must be diplomatic in your treatment of her.'

Charles beamed. 'Of course, sir, I shall be as tactful as possible,' he said. I wondered how tactful that would be.

After we had been given our orders for the week, the Vicar said, 'Secombe, I want you to go and make some enquiries on my behalf for the Soldiers, Sailors and Airmen Family Association. As you probably know, they look after families of servicemen when they are in need. There's the wife of a deserter living in twenty Maes-y-Coed Avenue near St Padarn's – name of Morris.'

'I know the children,' I replied. 'They come to Sunday School.'

'Do they?' asked the Vicar. 'Will you call there this afternoon and then let me know their circumstances?'

I decided to pay a visit to Mrs Morris in the early afternoon to avoid embarrassing Matthew who would be in school. Maes-y-Coed Avenue consisted of council houses built in the 'thirties. Already it had all the appearance of a slum. I walked through the jungle of weeds which represented the front garden of number twenty and knocked on the front door.

Two of the panes in the window of the room downstairs had been replaced by pieces of cardboard.

There was no response to my knock. I knocked again much harder. I heard sounds of movement and then footsteps on the uncarpeted concrete floor of the hallway. A large unkempt lady in her early thirties opened the door, inadequately covered in a pinafore like Annie Jones' neighbour. She looked ill at ease.

'Yes?' she asked.

'I've come from S.S.A.F.A.,' I said. 'I understand you are in need of help.'

'You'd better come in, Reverend,' she replied.

She led me into the front room. There was a strong smell of tobacco smoke mingling with other none too pleasant aromas, which had accumulated since the cardboard had replaced the two empty panes.

'Please sit down, Reverend,' she said. I placed myself in an armchair whose rexine covering had suffered from the attentions of the children. Moreover, the springs provided an unexpected hazard for the sitter. Mrs Morris remained standing, nervously doing a mime of washing her hands.

'I understand that your husband has deserted from the Army and that you are in need of financial and other assistance.' I was beginning to sound like a man from another kind of ministry.

'Yes, he – er – left his barracks about a month ago.' She was obviously on edge. 'It's very awkward without his allowance coming – I've got two kids in school.'

'Matthew and Ben,' I said. 'They come to Sunday School.'

'Oh, you're Mr Secombe then. They've talked about you. Pleased to meet you.' She thrust a grubby hand into mine.

There was a half-suppressed male cough from the kitchen. Mrs Morris looked distinctly embarrassed.

'How are the children off for clothing, shoes and so on?' I knew they were badly off, but I wanted the information from her own lips.

'Well, you know what growing children are, Reverend. Matthew is through his shoes for a start and 'e'll 'ave to 'ave another pair of trousers. Ben is even worse, 'is shirt is sticking out of the ones 'e's got.'

'What about money?'

'You can imagine 'ow much you get from the National Assistance. 'Ow they expect you to live, I don't know.' Her indignation was transformed into acute nervousness when a fit of smoker's coughing emanated from the kitchen.

'My – er – brother has come to see me,' she stammered in explanation. ''E won't come out from the kitchen till you're gone. 'E's – er – very shy.'

By now I was convinced that her husband was in the kitchen. She did not give the impression that she entertained other gentlemen in her husband's absence.

I stood up. It was a relief to escape from the spring in the chair. 'I'll see what can be done for you, Mrs Morris,' I said. 'The Vicar will be sending a report to headquarters. I expect you'll be hearing very shortly.' Then I raised my voice. 'I hope your husband will give himself up as soon as possible. You're going to suffer as a family until he does. Poor Matthew had to put up with having his father called a deserter in Sunday School yesterday.'

Mrs Morris's face was the same colour as the dirty white pinafore she was wearing.

'Thank you, Reverend,' she murmured, looking everywhere, except at me.

She saw me to the door and closed it, to her evident relief, behind me.

After visiting various houses on the list I had been given by the Vicar, I decided I had better give him the information about Mrs Morris before going back to my 'digs'.

I told him about my conviction that the deserter husband was hiding in the kitchen.

'I shouldn't be at all surprised,' said the Vicar. 'There are lots of Morrises. Sometimes they desert because they miss their wives and families. Generally it's because they can't stand Army discipline or they want to dodge overseas service. From what you say about the state of the house, it can't be desertion for love and care of his family. He won't stay there, don't you worry. He'll either disappear and his family will see him no more, or he'll give himself up. After all, the War's over now. He won't be treated too harshly.

'To be honest, Vicar,' I replied. 'I did suggest in a very loud

144

voice that he should give himself up. He must have heard that if he was in the kitchen.'

'Very commendable on your part,' commented my superior – a rare compliment.

A happy Charles Wentworth-Baxter was waiting for me when I returned.

'I'm going to stay with the Howells tonight,' he announced. 'You're right, they seem delightful people and I'm sure they'll make me feel at home. Thank you for your help this morning.'

'Don't mention it,' I said. 'What happened with Mrs Powell?'

'Believe it or not,' replied my colleague, 'the old dragon was not breathing fire after all. I think she was relieved that I was going. She probably did not want me there in the first place.'

'You're a lucky man, Charles,' I said. 'I think you'll find you've fallen on your feet among the fruit and veg.'

'Perhaps we can go and celebrate on my day off,' suggested the liberated prisoner.

'Provided the boss doesn't load me with work that day,' I replied.

He went off grinning like a Cheshire cat.

Mrs Richards was in similar mood when I joined her for tea.

'I've got a surprise for you,' she announced. 'I've given the bathroom that flick of paint that it needed. It's really been reformed. So I've got the boiler lit for you to have a bath tonight to celebrate.'

'That's two celebrations for me to join in,' I said. 'I wonder what the third will be.'

'What's the first one?' enquired my landlady.

'Charles has left Mrs Powell and he is going to stay with Moelwyn and his wife straight away. So he has asked me to join him in a celebration on his day off.'

'I'm very glad about that.' she said. He'll find Myfanwy Howells a different pot of tea from Mrs Powell. By the way, if he's taking you out for a celebration, I hope he'll do something about his appearing. He still looks like an old tramp about the place.'

'Maybe Myfanwy Howells can do something about that,' I replied.

'Yes,' said Mrs Richards, 'she's as neat as two pins.'

A few hours later, after my landlady had gone to bed, I decided that the time had come to enjoy the comfort of a hot bath in the 'reformed' bathroom.

I divested myself of my clerical uniform and put on the battered dressing-gown which had covered me throughout five years of college life. My landlady had achieved wonders with the hot water, which came boiling out of the tap. I locked the door, hung up my dressing-gown on the hook, tested the bath temperature and lowered myself gently into the steaming water. I always sit in my bath for a few minutes before lying in it. I like the water to be so hot that it needs a gradual approach to complete immersion. On this occasion my routine was providential.

When I went to reach for the soap, which reposed on a rack near the taps, I found myself unable to raise my posterior. I was firmly anchored by fresh paint to the bottom of the bath! After several painful attempts to dislodge myself I decided to wait until the water cooled. I thought that perhaps the heat of the water had melted the fresh paint.

However, as the water cooled there was no sign that I was becoming unstuck. I began to panic. I had visions of myself being taken to the fire station in a bath – a Reverend Diogenes. Although the water was now tepid, I was sweating profusely.

'Mrs Richards,' I yelled. She was somewhat deaf and was probably asleep. 'Mrs Richards!!!' I banged on the side of the bath. At least the paint there had dried. There was silence when I stopped shouting. The water was getting cold. I began to shiver. 'Help!' I shouted and banged with my fist as hard as I could on the side of the bath. Suddenly my banging on the bath was augmented by a banging on the door. It was the relief of Mafeking.

'Anything wrong?' The plaintive voice of an anxious Mrs Richards was like music to my ears.

'I'm stuck to the bath,' I said.

'What?' She sounded bewildered.

'Stuck to the bath!' I was now so desperate that my voice was almost falsetto.

'Must be the paint,' she said.

'I know it's the paint,' I was fighting to retain my sanity. 'I can't move.'

'Don't worry. Keep your chin down. I'll go and get Mr Evans, next door.' The tone of alarm in her voice outweighed any reassurance she intended to give. 'You'll have to wait till I dress, though,' she added.

I moaned. The thought of waiting another ten minutes while Mrs Richards dressed and then proceeded next door to rouse a slumbering Mr Evans, impelled me to a final Herculean effort to escape from the paint. My numb buttocks strained at their anchorage. The Lord heard my prayer and I shot forward so rapidly that my nose well nigh jammed itself between the taps. But my bottom, a very painful, paint-anointed bottom, was in the air. I was intoxicated with relief. I jumped out of the bath, grabbed my towel and wrapped it around me. I opened the bathroom door and shouted joyously, 'Mrs Richards – it's all right. I'm free!'

Her bedroom door opened. It was a strange sight which emerged. My landlady's unbunned hair straggled around her face and her shoulders, while the rest of her was shielded by a voluminous nightdress which she held tightly to her bosom. 'Thank goodness for that,' she beamed. 'You haven't hurt yourself, have you?'

'It's just my posterior. I think I must have left some of my skin in the bath.' My bottom was extremely sore.

'I hope you're all right,' she said. 'That part of your anomaly can be very tender. Would you like me to have a look at it?'

'No, thank you, Mrs Richards,' I hastened to reply. 'But I should be grateful if I could have an ointment of some kind.'

'There's some ointment in the cupboard downstairs. It's for cuts. It's anaesthetic so it will kill any germs. I'll go and get it for you.'

By now, I had begun to shiver again. I disappeared into the bathroom and began to dry myself with some vigorous rubbing. A few minutes later there was a knock on the door.

'Here's the ointment, Mr Secombe.' Mrs K. sounded very solicitous.

I opened the door a few inches and received the precious balm, together with some cotton wool.

When I applied the ointment I was surprised to find a fair amount of blood on the cotton wool. The pain was increasing in intensity. If the ointment was 'anaesthetic' it was completely ineffective. Sleep was impossible. Much of the night, I spent walking around the bedroom. By the time dawn arrived, I knew that I should have to be first in the queue at the doctor's surgery that morning.

15

I must have been a ghastly sight when I came downstairs for breakfast. Mrs Richards stared at me.

'Mr Secombe,' she said, 'you do look dreadful. Is it your posterity?'

'It certainly is,' I moaned. 'I can't possibly sit down. I'll have to see the doctor.'

'I'm very sorry indeed,' apologised my landlady. 'I shouldn't have got your bath ready for a few days, till the paint had dried up. You'd better go straight away to the surgery. Then you'll be the first to see Doctor Hughes. He's always up to his neck in patients.'

The doctor's surgery was the end house of Melbourne Terrace. An annexe built at the side was the waiting-room. At eight forty-five a.m. I stood outside the door, alone and palely loitering. By nine a.m. I had been joined by a mixed bag of sickly people, ranging from bronchitic geriatrics to babes-in-arms.

At two minutes past nine the door was opened by the doctor's receptionist, a grey-haired lady in spectacles, who was rumoured to be better at diagnosis than the bumbling old physician. The sick folk of Pontywen showed remarkable agility in their fight to sit on the few chairs available.

'I'm afraid Doctor Hughes is away today,' announced the doctor's major-domo. 'There's a locum here instead.'

A number of the elderly surrendered their seats and went back home to wait for tomorrow.

The receptionist looked at me.

'I think you were first, Reverend,' she said and ushered me into the inner sanctum.

To my horror, behind the desk, was a pretty, dark-haired young lady about the same age as myself. She looked up from a sheaf of papers in front of her, fixed a pair of deliciously brown eyes on me, and said, with a smile, 'Sit down please.'

'I'm – er – afraid I can't,' I stammered.

'I see,' she replied, 'what is wrong with you?'

I was dying several thousand deaths.

'It's – er – my – er . . .' I didn't know whether to say 'posterior', which sounded coy, or 'buttocks', which sounded clinical. I decided on 'buttocks'.

She burst into peals of laughter which proved very contagious. My embarrassment disintegrated and I joined in the amusement.

'I'm sorry,' she said, 'that was very unprofessional. It was the look on your face rather than your buttocks. Now then, what's wrong with them.'

'Well,' I replied, 'it started with my landlady deciding to freshen up the bathroom with a "flick of paint", as she put it. In the course of which she painted the stained patches on the bottom of the bath.'

'Upon which you placed your bottom,' she interjected.

'Exactly,' I said. 'I filled the bath with piping-hot water and then sat down heavily on the fresh paint. In wrenching myself from the paint, I think I must have left some of my skin on the bath.'

'Drop your trousers then,' ordered the doctor. 'Don't worry – I have seen men's buttocks before – in the course of my training, I mean.' She stood up, a petite young lady, no more than a few inches over five feet and decidedly attractive.

I fumbled with my braces and my trouser buttons before eventually revealing my smarting bottom.

She whistled quietly. I would have liked to think it was in admiration, but knew that it was in commiseration.

'That looks quite nasty,' she said.

'It feels it,' I replied.

She went to the medicine cupboard and produced a bottle.

'This will make you jump when I apply it,' she warned, 'but it will kill any infection that may be there and start the healing process. It's going to take quite a while before the flesh heals.'

Gently she applied the lotion to my injured rump. It was a painful antidote but lost much of its venom due to the compassion of the applier.

'You can make yourself respectable again,' she ordered. 'You had better come back in a week's time for a check up. In the meantime, I'll make out a prescription for the lotion which you must apply morning and evening.'

As she was writing out the prescription, she said, 'How long have you been in Pontywen?'

'Just over four months,' I replied. 'And if I may ask, how long have you been doing a locum for Doctor Hughes?'

She finished her writing with a flourish and looked up at me. My pulse rate accelerated alarmingly.

'This is my first stint. Doctor Hughes is a friend of the family and rang me at the weekend to see if I would help out today. Between you and me, there is a possibility that I might be taken on as junior partner.'

'That would be wonderful,' I enthused. Then, greatly daring, I said, 'You see, I've always thought that the Church and medicine should work hand in hand. As one junior partner to another perhaps I might suggest we could get together to establish some kind of cooperation.'

'Hand in hand?' she enquired.

'Something like that.'

'Tell me . . .' she paused. 'I don't know your name.'

'I'm Fred Secombe.'

'I'm Eleanor Davies. Tell me, Fred Secombe, are you trying to date me or are your motives purely altruistic?'

'In a word, both. But mainly the first.'

'For a Curate, you're a fast worker.' She smiled.

I thought Mona Lisa would come a poor second in competition with Eleanor Davies. Within five minutes of meeting this young lady I was already besotted.

'You realise that there is a queue of patients outside while you are indulging in a flirtation with the doctor.' She wrote something quickly on a prescription pad. 'Take this prescription together with the other.'

She stood up and ushered me to the door.

'Next please,' she called.

Within seconds, I was out of the surgery examining the

second 'prescription'. On it was written, 'Ring me tonight after 8 p.m. Llangwyn 292.'

A startled elderly lady stared at a young Curate who shouted 'Whoopee!!' as he read his prescription outside the door of the surgery. Pontywen had become the greatest place on earth. I blessed Mrs Richards for painting the bath and Dr Hughes for engaging a locum. 'Bless 'em all' I began to whistle as I made my way back to my digs.

'My word,' said Mrs Richards when I came back, 'you're a lot better already. When you went out, I was getting ready for your internment. You looked so terrible.'

'It's all down to the doctor,' I replied and, catching hold of the old lady, tried to waltz her around the kitchen.

'What ever is the matter with you?' enquired my bewildered landlady.

'Doctor Hughes wasn't there this morning. He had a locum at the surgery and she's the most delicious locum ever invented. What's more, I have to telephone her tonight.' I was on cloud nine.

'So that's it,' said Mrs Richards. 'You've had the best medicine you can get. You've fallen in love by the sound of it. No wonder you've forgotten the pain in your sit-you-down. What's her name?'

'Her name is Eleanor. Isn't that a musical name?' I rhapsodised.

'What's her other name?' persisted Mrs R.

'Eleanor Davies and she lives in Llangwyn. Her father is a friend of Doctor Hughes.' I replied.

'Oh! That's Doctor Davies's daughter. Nice little girl. Went to Pontywen Grammar before she went to college.' Mrs Richards was a mine of information.

'So you know her,' I said in reverential tones.

'Well, I haven't seen her since she was in school. Her father used to be the other doctor in Pontywen, till he went to Llangwyn. Its a better class of practising up there.'

Llangwyn was a little market town some miles north of Pontywen. Not far from where Harry Tench's car had broken down.

At eight p.m. that evening I joined a queue outside the phone box in the town square. It was eight forty-five before I could enter the portals, by which time I was in a ferment of frustration and excited anticipation. The air inside the booth was heavy with cheap perfume and tobacco smoke.

After two false starts, I got through to Llangwyn 292. The female voice at the other end was calm and self-assured.

'Llangwyn 292.'

I took a deep breath. My voice trembled.

'Could I speak to Doctor Eleanor Davies?'

'You're speaking to her, Reverend Fred Secombe.' She was trying to suppress her amusement. 'Why so long before you have phoned me?'

'I have had to wait in a queue to get into the box.'

'All is forgiven. First of all, how is your bottom, or as you so charmingly put it, your buttocks?'

'Very painful, I'm afraid.'

'You must get your landlady to dress it tonight and apply the lotion.'

'I thought I would do it myself by using the shaving mirror in the bathroom.'

She burst into laughter.

'I don't think you could do that even if you were a contortionist. This is no time for false modesty. Your kindly old landlady will be only too pleased to help, I'm sure. If she were young, I wouldn't suggest it.'

'Now may I make a suggestion,' I said.

'I never thought curates could be suggestive.' She was mocking me again.

'Well this one is and my suggestion is that we meet somewhere next week on my day off. The D'Oyly Carte Company are in Cardiff. I thought perhaps we might have a meal and then go to the theatre.'

There was a pause the other end.

'Would you be more specific? When is your day off?'

'A week today; next Tuesday.'

'I have to take surgery for Doctor Hughes and attend to your bottom again, don't forget. But I could get away after evening surgery and pick you up at your digs. We could be in Cardiff by seven with a bit of luck.'

'Fantastic. I'll book seats tomorrow morning by phone.'

'That's if you can get them,' she said. 'D'Oyly Carte are

always fully booked. If they are, then we'll have to get up into the "gods". It will be better for you anyway. You'll be able to stand for the performance.'

'By the way,' I asked, 'do you like Gilbert and Sullivan? I should have asked you that first. People either love them or hate them.'

'I have been brought up on them.' she replied. 'My father is a G and S fanatic. He has most of their operas on records. What's more, I have sung quite a few of the soprano leads in college.'

'This is fate,' I burbled, only to be rudely interrupted by the pips. Frantically I searched in my pocket for another two pence. I always begin my search for anything in the wrong pockets. The phone went dead. A female face was pressed against the window of the box – a very annoyed female face. Confusion overwhelmed me. I was positive I had plenty of coppers. By now, I realised I had plenty of pockets, also. At last, I found the coins in my clerical waistcoat. I bestowed a wan smile on the face at the window – only to be greeted with a curl of the lips.

Once again I dialled Llangwyn 292.

'Hallo, Fate,' came the voice. 'What happened?'

'I'm afraid I couldn't find in what pocket I had put my coins.'

'You'll find it easier next time you phone me to put all your coins on tops of the box. Sorry for interrupting. You were saying?'

'I was about to say that your experience as a soprano lead at college is a stroke of fate. For the past few months, I have been thinking of starting a Gilbert and Sullivan group as a church activity in Pontywen, that is, if my lord and master agrees.'

'Which one is that? The one up above or the one in the vicarage?'

'Madame, you are teasing me. Speaking seriously, would you be interested in playing the lead in *Pirates*, for example?'

'I think we had better discuss this next week. My father has emerged from his lair and appears to need the phone. See you next Tuesday. Goodbye.'

Before I could say 'Goodbye' she had put the phone down.

154

As I emerged from the box, the head of the queue outside turned to the others behind her.

'About time, too,' she commented. I think it irked her that I was grinning so broadly.

When I got back to my digs, Mrs Richards informed me that Charles had called.

'He's very happy at the Howellses,' she said. 'He's like a bird with two tails. As tomorrow is his day off, he says he'll be here at seven o'clock for you two to go and have a bust up to celebrate.'

'I've got plenty to celebrate,' I proclaimed. 'Next Tuesday, Eleanor and I are going to Cardiff to the theatre.'

'Would you never!' she exclaimed. 'Mr Secombe you are fast at moving, aren't you?'

'What is more,' I continued, 'she said that it would be advisable for you to apply the lotion to my rear end, since I wouldn't be able to see what I was doing. So I should be very grateful if you would do that later this evening.'

'She sounds a very considerate young lady, thinking of your poor posterity like that,' said my landlady approvingly. 'Of course I'll comply the lotion. Just let me know when you're ready.'

At seven o'clock prompt next evening, Charles arrived, looking very pleased with himself. His appearance was much improved. He had a clean shirt; his hair had been brushed, perhaps even washed and the leather patches on the elbows of his jacket had been sewn securely. Evidently Myfanwy Howells was faster at moving than I.

'Where's your collar and tie then?' demanded Charles.

'It may be your day off,' I said, 'but it's not mine. I've no scruples about walking into a pub, wearing a clerical collar.'

'I thought we were going to have a real celebration,' moaned my colleague.

'If you mean by that, getting tight – as far as I'm concerned, that's out,' I pontificated. 'In any case, my one decent shirt is in the wash.'

'All right,' he said. 'Now then, where shall we go?'

'You're a fine one,' I replied. 'Inviting me to a night out and then asking me where we should go.'

'Come off it,' snapped Charles. 'You know this part of the world better than I do.'

'Peace be with you, brother,' I said soothingly. 'What about getting the train to Cardiff? We can't go drinking in this vicinity. If we do it's sure to get back to our reverend employer.'

Later that evening, as we stood at the bar counter in a pub in St Mary Street, Cardiff, I said to my colleague, 'What would you feel about me starting a Gilbert and Sullivan group in Pontywen?'

'I'd be all for it,' replied Charles. 'We used to do the operas in my school.'

Charles had gone to a public school. I had gone to a grammar school where once a year the pupils performed a Shakespearean play as the sole dramatic activity.

'I think I'll have a word with the Vicar tomorrow,' I said. 'I've produced some plays at college and I've sung some G and S at concerts. I'd love to do something like *The Pirates of Penzance*, both taking part and directing.'

'If you want a pianist, I'll be glad to oblige,' Charles announced.

'This must be divinely ordained,' I enthused. 'Yesterday I find a leading soprano, today I find an accompanist.'

'Who's the leading soprano?' he asked.

'None other than the young lady with whom I have a date next Tuesday,' I said proudly.

'And who may that be?' Charles was now very interested.

'Doctor Eleanor Davies, whom God preserve, of Llangwyn,' I intoned.

'Good heavens!' he exclaimed. 'You are a high flier.'

'Last night Mrs Richards described me as a fast mover and now you as a high flier. They could do with me in the Air Force.' I felt very pleased with myself.

Next morning, we met at the vicarage for the mid-week palaver with Canon Llewellyn.

'Are you settling in at the Howells'?' said the Vicar to Charles.

'Oh yes!' gushed my friend. 'They are very kind people and I'm sure I'll be very happy there.'

'The proof of the pudding will be in the eating,' grunted the Vicar.

Charles looked like a punctured balloon.

I decided that it was not a propitious time to mention frivolities like Gilbert and Sullivan groups.

Then the old man turned to me. 'Secombe,' he said, with his head perched to one side and with one beady eye fixed on me. 'I have been thinking. It's time that St Padarn's had more independence. Now that the War is over and the boys will be back from the Forces, the church up there will be able to stand more on its own two feet. So I propose to give you sole charge, occasionally helping out in the parish church or St Illtyd's.'

God moves in a mysterious way His wonders to perform, I thought.

'Thank you very much, Vicar,' I replied. 'I should be delighted to take the responsibility. Does that mean that I shall have a free hand to organise the social aspect of church life in St Padarn's?'

'What are you getting at?' he asked suspiciously.

'Well, for example,' I paused, searching for suitable words, 'I should like to encourage non-church goers to join the faithful by setting up something like a Gilbert and Sullivan group.'

'I don't think Gilbert and Sullivan ever thought of themselves as missionaries,' said the Vicar. 'Still, if you want to start a group, carry on, Secombe. But, don't let that interfere with your real work – caring for souls.'

From that moment, Pontywen Church Gilbert and Sullivan Opera Company came into being.

16

The next day, there was one of those autumn mornings when it appears that the Almighty has put the calendar back to midsummer. The sunlight streamed into my room and drew me to the armchair in the bay window. I had just finished reading the weekly letter from my mother and had arrived at the inevitable PS from my father – 'Are you keeping your bowels open?' He had a deep conviction that constipation was the root of all evil.

Suddenly the sunlit silence was shattered by a noise which sounded like continuous machine-gun fire. I jumped to my feet to see an ancient Morris Minor draw up outside. With a heady mixture of surprise and delight I saw that the driver was none other than Dr Eleanor Davies.

By the time she had emerged from the car, I was out on the doorstep to greet her.

'You'd better be careful!' I warned her. 'Will Book and Pencil will have you for disturbing the peace.'

'Don't worry,' she said, 'when I take you to Cardiff the engine will be as quiet as a well behaved sewing machine. It's going to the garage this afternoon.'

'Would you care to come in?' I asked. I did a pale imitation of a Sir Walter Raleigh bow and arm flourish.

'No time, I'm afraid,' she replied. 'I'm on my way to the surgery. If you will stop doing the Romeo and Juliet balcony scene in reverse and come down here, I'll explain my errand.'

'Sorry,' I said. I cleared the two steps and landed at her side. 'In fact, I was trying to do a Sir Walter Raleigh.'

'Dismal failure,' she commented. 'I thought you were trying to do the Hunchback of Notre Dame. Anyway, enough of this badinage. A woman came to surgery last night with a black eye and injuries to her ribs. She said she had fallen downstairs.'

'What has that got to do with me?' I asked.

'It looks to me,' she replied, 'as if she has been beaten up by her husband who has just returned from the Forces. I think it's a case for you before it becomes a case for Will Book and Pencil.'

My mouth opened, but no sound emerged.

'That's a very good imitation of a goldfish,' she said.

'It's – it's – ' I stammered. 'Well, I've never tackled anything like this before.'

'There's always a first time,' said Eleanor sharply. 'You said that you thought the Church should work hand in hand with medicine. I've done my bit – now it's up to you.'

She was a forceful young lady.

'Right!' I said, suddenly full of resolution. 'What's her name and address?'

'That's more like it,' replied the apple of my eye. 'She's Mrs Evelyn Thomas, thirteen, Williams Terrace. She's about forty and she has three children, all at school.

'What about the husband?' I asked. 'Is he at home, or has he found work yet?'

'He started work at the steelworks. He was in the Welsh Guards,' came the reply.

I gulped. I was hoping he was five feet tall and a bantam weight.

'You – er – don't happen to know what shift he's on?' I enquired nervously.

'I was more concerned with the lady's injuries than her husband's work schedule,' she said. 'Why, what difference does that make?'

'It was only that it would be wise to see the lady when her husband wasn't there,' I replied.

'I would have thought it unwise to see ladies when their husbands aren't there,' she said archly.

'Believe it or not,' I retorted, 'in my job, I am forever seeing ladies in their husbands' absence.'

'Lucky you,' she commented. 'But you're quite right. It's just as well that you see her on her own. I suppose you'll have to take pot luck. If he's there this morning, then you can pay another visit this afternoon, when he'd be at work.'

'You're beginning to sound like my Vicar,' I remarked.

'As long as I don't look like him, I don't mind,' she said. 'I have to go. Phone me tonight and tell me what's happened.'

In seconds the car was off with such a noise that half a dozen doors opened in alarm. I sped into my digs.

The armchair in the bay window had become a hot seat physically and metaphorically. How on earth was I going to get the truth from Mrs Evelyn Thomas and, having got it, what was I going to do with it? As I sat and pondered, Mrs Richards knocked on my door.

'Would you like another cup of tea, Mr Secombe?' she enquired.

'No thank you,' I said, 'but I would like some information – if you've got it, that is.'

She beamed. The old lady loved to unstock her cupboard of information.

'Do you know a Mrs Evelyn Thomas, number thirteen, Williams Terrace?' I asked.

'Well, I don't know her to speak to,' she answered, 'but I know her by sight. A little woman with three little boys. Her husband's been debobbed. A big man – nasty. They do say he's given her a terrible time since he's back.'

'Why?' I said. 'Does he drink?'

'No, no', she replied, 'it's not drink. They say the War has made him a bit queer – you know – mentally inflicted.'

'They' featured a lot in Mrs Richards' information. I always found 'they' were well informed.

'Thank you very much, Mrs Richards,' I said. 'That's very helpful.'

She did not ask the reason for my questions. She never did. She beamed once again and left the room, happy to have obliged.

It took me half an hour to screw up enough courage to get up and go to thirteen, Williams Terrace. I sauntered rather than walked. All too soon I arrived at the house.

Bright clean curtains adorned the windows and the front door had been given a fresh coat of G.W.R. chocolate paint.

The house gave every impression of being 'Home Sweet Home'.

I drew in a large breath and knocked on the door. Seconds later, the front window curtain was moved a fraction to one side. Quickly the curtain was returned to its neat folds. I waited for the door to open. Nothing happened.

If I leave now, I said to myself, Eleanor will think I have chickened out. I knocked again, much more imperiously. After the third bout of knocking, I heard footsteps in the passage.

The door opened slowly to reveal a petite Mrs Thomas, neatly attired in jumper and skirt. Her thin sallow face was disfigured by a massive bruise which had closed her left eye.

'Sorry to be so slow answering the door,' she said. Her voice trembled. 'I was upstairs, doing the beds.'

'I'm the Curate at St Padarn's,' I announced.

'I know,' she said. 'It's Mr Secombe, isn't it?'

'That's right,' I replied. 'I'm visiting the street. Would you mind if I came in and had a chat?'

She looked very agitated.

'Well, I don't know,' she said. 'I've got to go out shopping in a minute.'

'If you could spare a little time, I'd be grateful,' I replied.

'Oh, all right then,' she murmured. 'Mind, I can't stop long talking.'

She ushered me into the front room. It smelt of furniture polish. The linoleum shone between the cheap rugs which were placed in perfect symmetry on it. For a house which contained three young children, it appeared remarkably tidy. A photograph of a Welsh Guardsman stood in splendid isolation on the mantelpiece.

'Is that your husband?' I asked.

'Yes,' she said. 'He's demobbed now. He do work in the steelworks. That's why I've got to go out shopping – to get his dinner. He's working six to two and he do like his dinner on the table when he comes home.'

Talking about her husband made her even more agitated.

'Any children?' I enquired.

'I've got three boys,' she replied. 'The oldest is eleven and the others are eight and six years old. They're good boys really.'

'What about Sunday School for them?' I said. This suggestion seemed to frighten her.

'No!' she exclaimed. 'It's my husband. He wouldn't allow it. He's gone against religion since he's been in the Forces.'

'That's all right, Mrs Thomas,' I said soothingly. 'I don't want to cause any trouble between you and your husband. You seem to have enough to worry about with the nasty accident you must have had.'

'It's a fall I had yesterday,' she said. 'I slipped at the top of the stairs and fell to the bottom. I've been to the doctor. She was very good. She bandaged my ribs and I've got some tablets.' She paused. 'If you'll excuse me, I've got to go out now.'

She led me to the door. On the doorstep we shook hands as two interested neighbours looked on.

'I'll call again perhaps,' I said.

She said nothing but closed the door quickly.

As I made my way back to my 'digs', I wondered how I was to tell Eleanor that I had been so ineffective.

'You don't seem to have much of an appetite today,' commented Mrs Richards at the dinner table. 'It must be that old love sickness that's doing it. Either that or some stomach ailment.'

'It's neither,' I replied. 'I've got an awkward problem on my mind and I can't see any solution to it.'

'Don't worry, Mr Secombe,' she said. 'All those clouds have got silver inside them.'

It was my afternoon for hospital visiting. All the time I was there I kept thinking that Mrs Thomas would be one of the patients soon, if nothing was done. To add to my misery I was attacked by a bout of toothache in the Princess Royal Ward. It was so violent that I cut short my ministrations and went back to my 'digs'.

I took some aspirins and went up to my bedroom. I lay on my bed and prayed for the balm of sleep. In no time my pains were lost in the land of Nod. However, that peaceful land was invaded by a horde of bellowing Nazi storm troopers. They were advancing on me with bayonets at the ready. I awoke in a frightened sweat.

To my horror, I could hear a man's voice in the house making more noise than all the storm troopers put together. I jumped off the bed. Half dazed I made my way to the landing. There at the bottom of the stairs was a giant of a man towering over the little figure of Mrs Richards.

As soon as he saw me he shouted, 'Come down 'ere. I want to 'ave words with you.'

Still drowsy, I descended the stairs, hanging on to the banisters and slipping in my stockinged feet on the polished linoleum. Mrs Richards had interposed her small frame between the invader and the bottom step.

'I'm sorry, Mr Secombe,' she said in trembling tones, 'but he pushed his way in.'

'It's all right,' I assured her. Then addressing the hulk, I found myself saying, 'Perhaps you would like to come into my room.'

He barged his way past me into the front room and I closed the door.

'My name's Thomas,' he announced 'You've been 'aving – er – relations with my wife while I've been away fighting for my Country.'

I heard the front door close. Through the side window I saw Mrs Richards do a flying descent of the steps, worthy of someone a quarter of her age.

'Sit down, Mr Thomas,' I said, making a vain attempt to be in charge of the situation.

'Sit down yourself,' he replied and pushed me into my armchair. he was a gorilla of a man, bursting his new demob suit at its seams.

'I'm not going to hurt you,' he growled, 'as long as you do as I ask. All I want is a signed confession.'

'But, Mr Thomas,' I protested, 'I have had nothing to do with your wife. I never met her until this morning.'

'Don't lie to me,' he shouted. 'Now get some paper and write that down.'

I decided to stall for time, hoping Mrs Richards would come soon with the relief of Mafeking.

'Look, Mr Thomas,' I said. 'I'll have to go upstairs for paper. I've used up everything here.'

'Don't try that with me,' he hissed.

He produced a pencil from his pocket. 'Now then,' he said, through clenched teeth. 'Write it down on that paper.'

He brought me *The Times* which lay on the table.

I took the pencil and stared at the front page. Painfully conscious of the menacing presence above me, I put down the pencil.

'I'll have to find a clear space to write on,' I said. 'This front page is too full of print.'

With trembling hands I opened the newspaper. As I did so, I heard the hurried sound of footsteps in the street. In no time at all, Will Book and Pencil's burly figure came up the steps of number thirteen, a helmeted angel of the Lord.

'You've sent for the police, you rat,' shouted the ex guardsman. He dashed out of the room and made for the back door. I went to the front.

'He's gone out through the back door, I think,' I said in a shaky voice.

'You all right?' asked the policeman.

'I'm OK, thank God,' I said. 'You know who it is; Thomas, thirteen, Williams Terrace.'

'I know,' he replied, 'Mrs Richards told me. I'll go along to the house.'

A few minutes later, my landlady appeared, as white as a sheet.

'Are you all right, my dear?' she asked, gasping for breath.

'I'm fine,' I said and gave her a hug.

'Mr Secombe!' she breathed. 'We're on the doorstep. What will the neighbours say?'

Once inside my room, she explained that she was on her way to the police station when she met Will Book and Pencil.

'Fair play,' she said. 'He was off before you could say Cock Robin.'

I told her the whole story from Eleanor's visit to my visit in Williams Terrace and the scene in my room.

'Well,' said my landlady, 'it's what I always say. Never interfere between Man and Wife. Your young lady will find that out in time.'

Later that evening I made my way to the phone box in the square and took my place in the queue. After waiting half an hour I got through to my 'young lady'.

'What's happened?' she demanded.

'You might well ask that,' I said with a fair amount of vehemence.

'Why?' asked Eleanor in muted tones.

'It's just that my errand of mercy almost produced a violent attack upon my person,' I said.

There was a silence at the other end.

'I'm sorry,' she murmured. 'I think you had better explain.'

When I had finished, she exclaimed, 'The man needs psychiatric treatment. So does she if she has made such an allegation. It's probably not true.'

'In that case, how did he come to have my name?' I shouted.

'Calm down, dear boy,' she said quietly. 'Perhaps a stupid neighbour mentioned to him that they had seen you go into the house, that would be enough for a man in his mental state.'

'Come to think of it,' I said, 'there were two old dears who saw me when I came out of the house.'

'That could be it,' she replied. 'Look, I'm horrified that I have landed you in this. I'll make it up to you next Thursday.'

Nightingales sang in Pontywen Square.

'I can't wait,' I said.

'Till then,' she breathed and hung up.

I emerged from the kiosk, floating on cloud nine. When I reached thirteen, Mount Pleasant View I was still travelling at the same ethereal level.

'You've got the colour back in your cheeks,' said Mrs Richards, 'Will Book and Pencil has been. He's coming back in half an hour.'

The constable was full of concern for my welfare when he arrived.

'Sorry about your trouble, Mr Secombe,' he boomed. 'It's not very nice to be threatened by a big bully like that. Mind I don't think he'd have hit you. He'd rather hit his wife.'

'What I can't understand is why my name has been dragged into this?' I said.

'Oh! You're not the only one by any means. He'd got a list of men he was going to see and get them to sign a confession. He was just starting off on the list when he came to see you.'

'But how did he come to get this list?' I asked, completely bewildered.

'What it was, was this,' Will explained. 'He came back from the Forces with his head affected. He'd heard how some of the soldiers' wives had been – er – you know and he had made up his mind that his wife was the same. I'm sure she never did anything like that. She's a tidy little woman.'

'I agree,' I said. 'She seemed to me to be the kind of person who would keep herself to herself.'

'Anyway,' he went on, 'he kept accusing her and beating her to get the names of all the men she was supposed to have been with. This afternoon when he came home from work he started on her again. She'd had enough by then. She told him she'd give him a list.'

'Did she indeed?' I interjected.

'She sat down and wrote it out,' said the policeman. 'She put down the names of men who would be the last to do anything like that. She put you down first, because you were fresh in her mind. Then she had Mr Evans, the minister at Calfaria, Councillor Waters and people like that. She thought it would make him see how stupid it was for him to suspect her. But the next thing she knew was that he'd put on his best suit and gone out.'

'So what's going to happen now?' I asked.

'Well, I've warned him about his conduct,' said Will Book and Pencil. 'Don't worry, you won't have any more trouble. It's his wife I'm sorry for. The man needs treatment. It's up to the doctor now.'

I started to laugh.

The police officer looked alarmed.

'That's the shock coming out,' he said, 'You'd better have a hot cup of tea with a lot of sugar and then have some aspirins after. Otherwise you won't sleep tonight.'

I had neither but I slept like a rock.

17

'It's time Miss Bradshaw had a visit.' Obviously the Vicar was in a sadistic mood when he gave me that task at the morning briefing. Any visit to Miss Bradshaw was an ordeal.

The old lady in question lived in a foul-smelling slum in Bevan's Row. Whiskery, unwashed, and unkempt, she was a source of fun to the children and a trial to the adults in the street. The house was overrun with cats. They were perched on the table, the chairs and any other available furniture – everywhere except on the floor.

Smoke from an unswept chimney filled the downstairs rooms. In the words of St Paul, the rare visitor would 'see through a glass darkly'. Sulphur, cats and stale boiled fish-heads combined to produce an unforgettable odour.

That afternoon I followed the usual routine for a Bradshaw visit. After one rap on the filthy knocker I opened the door and shouted, 'Miss Bradshaw!' The next step was to make my way to the middle-room door, through the passage. This was no mean feat because it entailed a journey between bundles of old newspapers, piled high on either side.

I knocked on the middle-room door and, according to the ritual, shouted once again 'Miss Bradshaw!' There was no reply. I opened the door gingerly.

To my horror, through the fog, I could see the figure of the old lady, lying in front of the fireplace. A bright fire glowed in the grate where a saucepan of fish-heads made their presence smelt.

The first thought that entered my head was the possible need of the kiss of life. Immediately I felt sick.

Slowly I approached the body. I prayed that it was still breathing. To my intense relief I heard a groan. I knelt beside her. The odour was so bad that it would have made eau de Full-Back Jones resemble a bunch of violets. Her eyes were closed.

'Are you all right?' I asked.

There was no reply.

'You idiot,' I said to myself.

Then I decided I would feel her pulse. Some five years previously, as a student, I had obtained a first aid certificate. It was awarded by a sympathetic examiner, who had passed the whole group.

Either I was holding her wrist in the wrong way or she was dead. Since she was breathing I came to the conclusion that I must be holding her wrist in the wrong way.

'The next step,' I informed myself, 'is to go for help.'

I dashed out of the house and knocked next door. An elderly lady appeared. She was wearing a dirty old raincoat and sporting a man's flat cap. Two wide eyes stared at me out of a coal-blackened face.

'It's Miss Bradshaw,' I blurted. 'She's collapsed. Will you stay with her while I go for the doctor?'

I did not wait for an answer. I left the startled occupant gawping on her doorstep.

The doctor's surgery was three streets away. I ran through them, like a bat out of heaven. When I turned the corner to the doctor's house, there was Eleanor's car standing outside.

I jumped the steps, two at a time. Before I could press the door-bell button, my beloved opened the door.

'What on earth is the matter?' she asked anxiously. 'You look ghastly and you're breathing like a grampus whale.'

'It's Miss Bradshaw!' I gasped.

'Who the hell is Miss Bradshaw?' she demanded, 'And what is the matter with her?'

'She's – er – an old lady who has collapsed,' I managed to say between gulps.

'Hop in the car,' she ordered, 'and wait till I get my bag. You're lucky. I was just about to go home.'

I hopped in, still panting. In seconds Eleanor was beside me.

'You look as if you are about to collapse, my dear,' she said, throwing her bag on the back seat. 'Now, tell mother all about it.'

As the car moved off, I launched into the case history.

'Miss Bradshaw lives in a slum . . .'

'That's good for starters,' she interjected.

'What's more,' I went on, 'she is surrounded by cats. There must be twenty cats or more.'

'Never mind the cattery,' she said impatiently. 'Come to the point, Frederick.'

'In a nutshell,' I replied in high dudgeon,' I went to visit her this afternoon and found her unconscious on the floor. I've left the next door neighbour with her.'

'I take it that she's breathing,' said Eleanor.

'Oh! Yes!' I answered. 'I thought I might have to give her the kiss of life but she groaned as I approached her.'

'What a devastating effect you have on elderly ladies,' she said. 'That's through doing your visits in a nutshell. In any case, you must save all your kisses for me.'

My dudgeon disappeared at lightning speed.

'This is it,' I said, as we turned into Bevan's Row.

'Here we go again,' commented Eleanor. 'Hand in hand, Church and medicine. I hope you are not chased by a madman this time.'

The front door was open, as I left it.

'Phew! What a dump!' she said. 'This passage looks like the trenches, World War One.'

Inside, the next door neighbour, with blackened face, still clad in cap and raincoat, was sitting on a chair, guarding the recumbent Miss Bradshaw.

'I think she's still breathing, Doctor,' whispered the neighbour.

'Get these moggies out of here,' commanded Eleanor in a voice worthy of a Sergeant Major, 'and try and open that window, if you can.'

The 'moggies' got the message before I could move into action. They stampeded towards the back door. I carved my way through a carpet of feline flesh and opened the door. The cats fled like a pack of lemmings in the suicide season.

When I returned to the middle room, the young lady doctor was on her knees at the side of the old lady, stethoscope at the ready.

'Leave the window for the time being,' she said to me, 'and go and phone for an ambulance.'

'Lewis, top shop, at the end of the street do have a phone,' announced the neighbour.

On my way there, I nearly knocked over Full-Back Jones. He had just come out of the local bookie's house.

'You're in an 'urry, young man,' he said.

'I've got to phone for an ambulance for Miss Bradshaw. She's had a heart attack or something,' I gasped.

'More work for us by the sound of it,' he said cheerfully. He added to my breathlessness with a forceful dig in the ribs.

Mr Lewis, short, thin, elderly and moustached was very accommodating. He was also very talkative. He led me through a maze of biscuit tins, relics of pre-War years. The phone reposed upon a column of empty Peak Frean tins.

'It's nine nine nine you want,' he instructed.

As I dialled, he said, 'Say you want the ambulance.'

I did so.

'Hold on,' said the operator.

'Serious then, is it?' asked Mr Lewis. The ends of his moustache were waxed. They gave him an air of spurious authority.

'Seems to be serious,' I said.

'I'm not surprised,' he replied. 'Never eats anything. Gives it all to the cats. That house must be full of germs. Like a pigsty. Catsty, rather.'

Mr Lewis guffawed.

'I'm afraid it's not funny, Mr Lewis,' I said. 'The old lady could be dead by the time I get back.'

'No wonder – the time they're taking to answer you.' He was quite unrepentant.

'You're through now,' said the operator.

'Can you send an ambulance to eleven, Bevan's Row?' I asked.

'This isn't a taxi service,' snapped a female at the other end. 'Who needs one and why?'

'It's an old lady who has collapsed – a Miss Bradshaw,' I said. 'She's unconscious. The doctor has come and sent me to phone for an ambulance.'

'That address again, please.' The tone of voice had changed.

'Eleven, Bevan's Row,' I replied.

'They'll be there as soon as possible,' announced the ambulance spokeswoman.

'What did they say?' enquired Mr Lewis, wiping his hands in his grocer's apron.

'They'll be there as soon as possible,' I said.

'How soon is possible, Reverend?' commented the shopkeeper.

'We'll have to wait and see,' I replied.

'You're going now then, are you?' he asked as I moved away between his biscuit tins. He sounded disappointed that I was not staying for a chat.

'I have to get back at once,' I said. 'Thank you for the use of the phone.'

'There's no charge,' he called out as I reached the door. 'I don't charge for emergencies.'

When I arrived at eleven, Bevan's Row, Eleanor was alone with Miss Bradshaw. The window was open and the saucepan had been removed from the fire. Fresh air was fighting a winning battle with fug.

'I've sent the female Al Jolson back home,' she said. 'That woman's been vaccinated with a gramophone needle. I'm afraid this poor old lady's heart is in a bad state. Her pulse is very faint.'

'I know,' I replied, 'I tried to find it and couldn't.'

'It's always in the same place – on the wrist, Frederick,' she said. 'I can see I shall have to give you lessons in first aid.'

'I have a certificate,' I boasted.

'They must have been giving them away,' she retorted.

'They were,' I admitted.

'Your Miss Bradshaw has neglected herself beyond words,' said Eleanor. 'She's badly undernourished, and when I examined her body it was almost as black as her neighbour's face.'

'Like Frederick the Great of Prussia,' I said.

'What about him?' she asked. 'He wasn't a negro, was he?'

'Of course not,' I replied, 'but it is said that when they came to prepare his body for burial, they found it was ebony black.'

'I bet your mother didn't know that when she gave you your name,' she said. 'From now on I think I shall call you "Stinker".'

'Over my dead body!' I expostulated.

172

'No,' she replied. 'Over his.'

With that the ambulance arrived and her banter gave place to a professional manner worthy of a more experienced physician. In a matter of minutes, Miss Bradshaw had been transported, still unconscious, into the ambulance.

'What happens now?' I asked.

'As far as I'm concerned, I have to go,' she replied. 'I am starving and my mother will be wondering where her little girl has gone.'

'I suppose I had better close the window and lock the doors,' I said.

'That's a very good idea,' replied Eleanor, 'and I can supply another one.'

'What's that?' I enquired.

'You can kiss me before I leave,' she said quietly.

I obliged.

'Practice is making you perfect,' she murmured. 'See you Wednesday evening. Be good.'

'That's my job,' I replied. 'Being good and doing good.'

'Big head!' she said and disappeared.

Before I could close the window half-a-dozen cats appeared from nowhere and leapt into the room via the window sill, like Grand National chasers. Now that Eleanor had gone, evidently they regarded me as a soft touch. Two of them proceeded to rub against my legs while the other four besported themselves on the furniture.

There was a tap on the front door. It was the 'female Al Jolson' who had turned into a fairy godmother. The coal dust had gone with the cap and the raincoat. In her neat blouse and black skirt she looked like the old lady in the Mazawattee tea advertisement, minus shawl.

'I'm sorry I was in such a state when you did call,' she said. 'I was getting in our load of coal from the colliery. My son's on the two till ten shift. So I had to do it by myself.'

'Has Miss Bradshaw any relatives?' I asked.

'None that I do know of,' she replied. 'She was an only child. Her father did have a cycle shop in the Square, until he went bust, like. Mind, May has always been a bit funny in the 'ead. It started when her sweetheart was killed in the War — the one before this last one, I mean. She spent all her time

reading the papers and feeding the cats. Never worked. She hasn't read any papers for years now, though. Once this last War started, that was it. Said it reminded 'er of the First War. So she just spends all 'er time with the cats. Why she do do it, I don't know.'

She paused for breath.

'I can see that she used to like reading the papers,' I said. 'What worries me is what is going to happen to the cats.'

'Well, Reverend,' she went on, 'I can tell you this. I'm not looking after them. What with the rations, it's all I can do to feed my son and myself. It's up to the Council to decide what they do do with them. And look at this house – the state it's in. My son do say that all these papers could start a fire and our house could go up with it. I don't like to say it but perhaps it's a Godsend that she's gone to hospital. Now the Council will have to do something. We've complained to them before about the cats and the papers. They said they couldn't do nothing because it wasn't a Council house. We'll see what they do do now.'

I decided on a quick exit to avoid another Niagara of words. It was obvious why Eleanor had got rid of her.

'Thank you for your help, Mrs . . .' I said.

'Williams.' She supplied the name at lightning speed.

'Mrs Williams,' I continued. 'Would you mind locking up and hanging on to the key? I'd better let the Vicar know what has happened to Miss Bradshaw.'

'What about the Council?' asked Mrs Williams.

'Perhaps the Vicar will have a word with them,' I said, only too pleased to pass the buck. 'He's got more pull then I have.' Then I escaped before she could begin another monologue.

The Vicar was mowing the lawn, his face purple with exhaustion. For someone in his late seventies, he was setting a furious pace – running, rather than walking, with the machine. However, while his little legs may have been in good condition, his bellows were decidely leaky.

'You've finished your visiting early,' he wheezed. He gave me a hostile glare from his one open eye.

'It's Miss Bradshaw, Vicar,' I said. 'I found her unconscious, lying beside the fireplace. She's just been taken to the hospital, I thought I had better let you know.'

'Humph!' he replied. Then he stared at the ground. There was a long silence, broken only by his wheezing.

'I've left the key with the woman next door, a Mrs Williams,' I said. 'She suggested that the Council might do something about the state of the house and all those cats.'

I had passed the buck.

'Phut!!' pronounced the Vicar and buried the buck.

'You had better get on with your visiting,' he snorted. Then he darted away in a stint of mowing and wheezing.

As I walked away from the Vicarage, I began to wonder whether I was in the right vocation. Faced with the Bradshaw situation, I had panicked, running wild around the streets of Pontywen. Eleanor and the Vicar were imperturbable. They were the 'Pros', I was the amateur. It was a disturbing thought.

I decided to bury it, alongside the buck. So I called on Idris the Milk and his missis. After a cup of tea and a tuna sandwich, God was in his heaven once again, and I was his accredited ambassador.

18

At St Padarn's on Sunday I announced that I was forming a Gilbert and Sullivan opera group. Immediately I put the cat among the nightingales by imposing an age limit for female members of the chorus. I had no desire to have grand-mothers masquerading as young ladies.

'No one over the age of thirty need apply,' I said.

The two leading sopranos of the church choir looked at each other with a mixture of astonishment and anger. Annie Jones had just replaced her false teeth after the last hymn. She opened her mouth so wide at the announcement that they were in danger of falling out once again.

'I'll help you out in the men's chorus,' said Bertie Owen. 'I used to be in the Penmawr Male Voice Choir.'

At that moment I wished I had put an age limit on the male chorus. Bertie's activities would be a sure guarantee of a blight on the whole production.

On Tuesday morning I was first in the queue at the doctor's surgery, waiting for the inspection by my beloved of my considerably improved ailment.

'Decidedly better,' she pronounced.

'I am sorry about the trouble I caused you,' I said.

'Not to worry,' she said, 'worse things happen at sea. Have you got seats for tonight?'

'We are lucky,' I replied. 'Two returned tickets for the circle.'

'Well, you should be able to sit through the performance by the look of your bottom. I'll treat you for the outing. I said I'd make it up to you.'

'No you don't,' I said firmly, 'I invited you; you can make it up some other way.'

'What on earth do you mean, you wicked clergyman,' she exclaimed in mock horror.

'Perhaps you might buy me a drink,' I answered with a grin.

'We'll talk about this later,' she said. 'In the meantime, carry on with the treatment. T.T.F.N.'

At six fifteen p.m. a dilapidated Morris Minor drew up outside thirteen Mount Pleasant View. I had been waiting at the window for some time, with a box of chocolates ready on the table.

'I'm going now,' I shouted to Mrs Richards.

She opened the middle-room door.

'Have a nice time at the Gilbert,' she said.

'I will, don't you worry,' I replied and ran down the steps, clutching the chocolates.

I thought Eleanor looked attractive in her white coat in the surgery. Now, as she stood outside the car, in a navy-blue two-piece suit, she looked magnificent – tiny, but magnificent.

'Hop in,' she ordered.

I hopped in and presented her with my month's sweet ration.

'You shouldn't have done that,' she said. 'It must have used up all your sweet coupons.'

'I'm not a great sweet eater,' I lied.

'By the way,' she said, as she threaded her way down the valley, 'have you got anybody in mind as musical director for your G and S?'

'I'm afraid not,' I replied. 'Everything's an act of blind faith. It seems to be working so far.'

'Well, it's going to work again.' She pulled up at a Halt sign. 'I think I can get you one.'

'You're a miracle worker!' I exclaimed and gave her a bear hug, colliding with the gear lever in the process.

'Disentangle yourself, Reverend,' she commanded, 'before we get booked by the police.'

'My apologies, madam.' I said. 'My excitement got the better of me.'

'Don't apologise,' she replied. 'It's just that the excitement came in the wrong place and at the wrong time.'

If she had taken my pulse at that moment, it would have broken the speed record for pulses.

'To get back to the musical director,' she went on. 'The music master at Pontywen Grammar School is a friend of mine. I'm sure I could persuade him to become your M.D.'

'Thank you very much,' I said, with as much enthusiasm as if she had offered me a spam sandwich.

'What's happened to your excitement?' she asked.

'Is he a – er – close friend, this music master?' I said.

'Jealousy will get you nowhere, Frederick,' she replied tartly.

'Mr Aneurin Williams is at least fifty, bald-headed and with a wife and six children. It just happens that he taught me music when I was in school and tried to persuade me to train at the Royal College of Music, instead of St Mary's Hospital, Paddington. What's more, young man, it's quite likely that he can get some of his senior pupils to join your Society.'

'Isn't life wonderful?' I enthused.

'You are an idiot,' she said and put her foot down hard on the accelerator.

At the theatre, I plucked up enough courage to hold Eleanor's hand halfway through Act Two of *HMS Pinafore*. It was a small hand but very responsive. By the finale we had established a close relationship.

She took my arm as we went back to her car.

'Just imagine,' I said, 'you could have been singing Josephine professionally.'

'I think I would rather be examining curate's buttocks professionally,' she replied.

'Do you mean I was not the first?' I asked.

'I specialise in such clerical examinations,' she said, 'but I must admit yours were the best.'

'When we arrived outside my digs, it was pitch dark.

'You may kiss me good-night,' she said briskly. 'And watch the gear lever this time.'

Never was an invitation so eagerly accepted. It was obvious that she was practised in the art of osculation as well as medicine. Her lips were soft and luscious.

'You might let me come up for air,' she exclaimed a

minute later. 'In any case, I think I had better be getting back.'

'Have I passed the clerical examination?' I enquired.

'For a Curate, you get top marks,' she declared.

'When do I see you again?' I said. 'I need to know about the music master and G and S.'

'That's your excuse,' she replied. 'Ring me at eight or thereabouts tomorrow night. Now I must go.'

Seconds later the Morris Minor sped away down the street. I stood on the doorstep savouring the delicate perfume which lingered on my overcoat. It was a decided improvement on the industrial aromas usually lingering around Mount Pleasant View.

When I got through to Eleanor next day, she was bubbling with enthusiasm. Aneurin Williams would be pleased to act as M.D. but he could only come on a Wednesday night at this stage.

'Fine by me,' I said.

'And by me,' she replied. 'I shall see that my Wednesday evenings are kept free.'

'Great!' I shouted. 'I'll go ahead and fix a meeting of all interested at St Padarn's for Wednesday of next week.'

'There's one other thing you'll be pleased to know,' said Eleanor.

'You can see me tomorrow?' I enquired.

'No, I can't,' she said firmly. 'It's just that Aneurin has a set of scores of *Pirates* from a school production before the War. He says you can borrow them.'

'Fantastic,' I replied, 'but qualified fantastic.'

'What do you mean?' she demanded.

'You can't see me tomorrow,' I explained.

'Blow, Blow, thou winter wind,' intoned Eleanor.

'All right,' I said, 'but I am grateful, deeply grateful. Honest. It's just that I should love to see you.'

'If you can hold your horses until Sunday evening,' she replied, 'perhaps we could meet after you have finished your one working day of the week.'

'I beg your pardon, madam,' I retorted. 'I work six days a week.'

'It all depends what you call work,' she said.

We met on the Sunday evening and consolidated the relationship.

'I must say,' she commented, after a prolonged embrace, 'I never knew that clergymen were subject to earthly passions.'

'A man is a man, whether he wears a dog collar or not,' I said. 'Some people get the idea that a dog collar is a compulsory halo which has every parson by the throat and chokes his manhood.'

'I must admit, I had the same illusion,' Eleanor replied. 'It's a pleasant surprise to find it proved false.'

'Shall I prove it again?' I asked.

'Please,' she said.

Next morning, a comparatively tidy Charles Wentworth-Baxter called for me at my digs. His landlady was fighting a winning battle with his appearance, although it was too early to say that it was decisive.

'Charles,' I enthused, 'you'll be pleased to know that next Wednesday the Pontywen Gilbert and Sullivan Opera Group is to be launched.'

'Wait a minute,' he said, 'that's my day off.'

My face fell a few inches.

'I had forgotten that,' I moaned. 'I suppose I'll have to look around elsewhere for a pianist.'

'What I could do,' he mused, 'is to ask the Vicar if I can change it to Thursday.'

Half an hour later at the vicarage a more than usually grumpy Canon Llewellyn was giving us our orders for the week.

When he had finished, Charles coughed nervously. 'Er – Vicar,' he stammered, 'would it be possible to – er – change my day off from Wednesday to Thursday?'

'Why?' snapped the Vicar.

'Well – it's because Fred is beginning his Gilbert and Sullivan rehearsals,' Charles replied. 'I've promised to play for them and they're being held on Wednesdays.'

The old man turned to me. There was a glint in his little eyes.

'Secombe,' he said, and paused. It sounded ominous. 'This missionary enterprise of yours,' he continued, 'could drive more people out of the church than it would bring into it.'

'What do you mean, Vicar?' I asked.

'Mrs Collier and Annie Jones have come to me, complaining that you have insulted them and some of the other ladies in the church,' he replied. 'You have deliberately excluded them from this venture of yours.'

My back was up immediately.

'I beg your pardon,' I said indignantly. 'I have not deliberately done anything of the sort. All I did was to say that I did not want anyone over thirty in the female chorus. We are going to perform the *Pirates of Penzance*. The ladies of the chorus are supposed to be the beautiful young daughters of General Stanley, not his maiden aunts.'

His head went to one side and one eye closed as he did his contemplative act. The seconds ticked by.

'There's a Welsh saying that the devil comes in with the formation of a choir,' said the Vicar. 'I should have remembered that when I gave you permission to go ahead. Well I've done it now, and I shan't go back on my word . . . It's up to you to deal with the ladies of St Padarn. They are not going to be easy to calm down.'

'I'll do my best, Vicar,' I assured him.

'What about my day off?' asked Charles.

'You must let me think about that,' said the Vicar enigmatically.

Back at Mount Pleasant View, Charles and I discussed the events of the morning over a cup of Mrs Richards' tea.

'I'll be there this Wednesday, day off or not,' said Charles.

'You'll get the day off changed,' I forecast. 'He's just being bloody. I don't think he's very well.'

'Come to think of it,' ruminated my colleague, 'he looked more purple than ever.'

At lunch I told Mrs Richards about the fuss Mrs Collier and Annie Jones had made about being excluded from the chorus.

'Don't worry about them, Mr Secombe,' she said. 'They won't leave the church over that. Even if they do, they're not indisposable. Nobody is, come to that.'

Charles and I were early at St Padarn's on Wednesday evening, arranging the benches and bringing out the antiquated piano from the vestry.

181

'This instrument will have to be tuned – or better still – replaced,' pronounced Charles.

A quarter of an hour before the rehearsal was due to begin, a dozen or so schoolgirls arrived, chattering excitedly. Evidently, Aneurin, the M.D., was a persuasive gentleman. Bertie Owen arrived with a young man in his late twenties, whom he introduced as, 'Iorwerth Ellis who can read music'.

By the time Eleanor came in with Aneurin Williams, the pair of them burdened with a pile of scores, there were thirty-six people present. Twelve men, including Idris the Milk and the other basses from the church choir, had turned up. For a society starting from scratch, it was a most encouraging number at a first rehearsal.

Aneurin, bald-headed, bespectacled and bandy legged, was short in stature but big in personality. His enthusiasm was infectious. After his five minute talk to the motley band of singers, they felt they were an operatic company already, without a note being sung.

Of the six tenors, only Iorwerth Ellis and myself could read music. The other four included Bertie who sat between Iorwerth and myself.

'We'll try out the tenors first,' said Aneurin, 'with cat-like tread! The accompanist will play the tenor line first and then I want all the tenors to come in on the beat.'

Charles hammered out the tenor line on the honky tonk piano. Aneurin winced. Iorwerth and I hummed the tune while the other four buried their heads in the score, quietly, as if to hide from the conductor.

'Now then,' said Aneurin, 'I want you to come in on three.'

Bertie turned over the pages of the score hurriedly to page three.

'What are you doing?' I asked him.

'He said, come in on three,' answered Bertie, 'but there isn't any music on that page – only the list of characters.'

'I thought you said you were in a male voice choir once,' I said.

'We didn't have anything like this book, only sheets of

paper with sol–fa,' Bertie replied. 'These birds on the wires – I can't follow them.'

'It's not just that,' I said. 'You must have had the conductor bring you in on the beat. That's why our conductor said, come in on three. One, two, three, start. That's what he meant, not turn to page three.'

'As far as I can remember,' said Bertie, 'our conductor used to say, "all together now" and raised his hand. Mind, that was twenty years ago and I only went twice.'

'That was when they found out why the choir had gone wrong all of a sudden, I suppose.' This remark from Iorwerth was intended to flatten Bertie.

It was Iorwerth's remark which fell flat, when Bertie replied, 'No, it wasn't that. I had to change my shift to nights. Mr Hughes, the conductor said it was a pity, because I had potential.'

'Perhaps he said it was providential,' said Iorwerth, trying out his devastating wit once again. I could see it was going to be difficult to decide who was the bigger headache – Iorwerth or Bertie.

'Can we start, please?' intervened Aneurin. 'Now then – one, two, three . . .'

A duet ensued between Iorwerth and myself. The other four sat in silence and wonderment. The M.D. was destined for a stint of hard labour.

By the end of the rehearsal, it was obvious that the chorus of young ladies was going to be a success in voice and appearance. It was equally obvious that the male chorus would have to be augmented, if the production was to be worthwhile.

After the chorus had departed, I turned to Aneurin. 'We'll have to get more men as soon as possible.'

'I'll see what I can do,' he said.

'You've already done more than your share,' I replied. 'I can't thank you enough.'

'Not at all, my dear boy,' he assured me, 'I'm only too pleased to be doing something like this.'

'Would you mind waiting outside?' said Eleanor to Aneurin. 'I'd like a few words with Mr Secombe in private.'

'I think I'd better go as well,' announced Charles. 'Two's company.'

As soon as they had gone, she came up to me and kissed me lightly on the mouth.

'I have news for you,' she said. 'Doctor Hughes has asked me to be his junior partner in Pontywen, and I've accepted at once, before he can change his mind. So Church and medicine can now go hand in hand good and proper.'

I put my arms around her.

'I love you,' I said.

'I'm glad,' she murmured, 'because they're my sentiments too.'

'In that case,' I asked, 'would you mind expressing them in three words?'

'*Je t'aime,*' she replied. 'I love you, persistent clergyman.'

We indulged in a protracted embrace.

'I'd better get back to Aneurin and take him home,' she said.

'But what about us?' I enquired.

'We both know about us now, my dear,' replied Eleanor. 'I'll be in touch.' She darted towards the door and blew me a kiss before disappearing.

My head spun. Events were moving at the speed of an express train. A few weeks ago, I was very much the junior Curate, unattached, a green apprentice in holy orders. Since then, I had become a senior Curate, with the responsibility of a church, the founder of an operatic group, and now, a lover, passionately attached to his doctor.

When I arrived back at Mount Pleasant View, my thoughts were still in a whirl of happiness. As I closed the front door, Mrs Richards emerged from the middle room, looking unusually sombre.

'Don't take your coat off,' she said. 'I'm afraid there's some bad news. The Vicar's had a heart attack. Mrs Llewellyn phoned up Thomas the paper shop to ask if you'll go at once to the Vicarage. It sounds as if it's the curtains for him, poor man.'

My landlady was right. By the time I reached the vicarage, 'the curtains' had closed on the life of Canon R. S. T. Llewellyn.

Doctor Hughes was leaving as I arrived. 'I'm afraid your Vicar has passed away,' he said, through the open car-window.

'I've given Mrs Llewellyn a sedative. She's in a state of shock. She'll need all the support you can give her, young man. Apparently, she has no close relatives, nor close friends, if it comes to that.' He looked over his gold-rimmed spectacles at me. 'By the way,' he added, 'I understand that you and Eleanor Davies are in the middle of a whirlwind romance. I think you should know that her parents don't approve. As far as I'm concerned, I don't think it advisable for my new junior partner to be otherwise engaged, as she begins her medical career. In any case, it looks as if you are going to have your hands full in the months that lie ahead.' So saying, he pressed the starter and drove off.

It looked as if the train of events was moving at such a speed that it was in danger of hurtling off the track.

The widow opened the door to me and ushered me into the lounge. She motioned me to sit down. Her face was ashen. Even her thin-lipped mouth looked drained of colour.

'This would never have happened if he had retired,' she said quietly. 'He would carry on. The Bishop didn't help by giving him that young man to train as well as you. It was too much.' There was a hint of a tear in her eyes.

'I'm very sorry for you, Mrs Llewellyn.' I found words difficult. 'As for the Vicar, I suppose, in one way, it was fitting that he should die in harness.'

'A harness is for a horse or a donkey,' she replied. 'It was the donkey work that killed him – and for what? So that somebody like John Whittaker can come and reap the benefit for his own glory.'

John Whittaker was an ambitous man in his early forties. He would be the last man I would wish to have as my Vicar. The very idea of it was a nightmare.

That night, as I lay in bed, my mind was in a turmoil. Three hours ago, I had been on the pinnacle of happiness. Less than an hour later, I had fallen from that height into a well of misery. My thoughts went back to the day when I arrived at the station in Pontywen, to be met by the comic little figure in his cloak and battered trilby. I wondered what he would advise me to do. 'He would carry on,' complained the widow. Then I remembered his rasping word of command at the station, 'Carry on, Secombe.'

Of course, that would be his advice, I said to myself. I determined I would carry on – regardless of Doctor Hughes, Eleanor's parents or even John Whittaker, if the worse came about. The rest I would leave to the Almighty – and, of course, Eleanor. An invincible combination.